C000233948

DEATH OF A SECRETARY

Trudy Thornton's body was run over by a lorry on the A12 in the early hours of the morning and DCI Millson and DS Scobie found their attempts to find her killer hampered by the secretive nature of the dead woman. One suspect is her boss, Charles Howard, an Under Secretary of State in the Home Office; another is the taxi driver she was friendly with who usually picked her up when she was late coming home.

But then there is a second murder and this time the strange and unpredictable Habenhowe twins are involved. Millson feels sure that the two murders are linked, particularly as the Habenhowe girls had provided one of his suspects with a false alibi for Trudy's murder. But even when Millson identifies the killer he cannot be sure that he will be able to secure the evidence before his adversary destroys it.

BY THE SAME AUTHOR

A FATAL REUNION
THE BOOK LADY
A COUSIN REMOVED
WITHOUT A TRACE

DEATH OF A
SECRETARY

Malcolm Forsythe

HarperCollins*Publishers*

Collins Crime
An imprint of HarperCollins*Publishers*
77–85 Fulham Palace Road, London W6 8JB

First published in Great Britain
in 1996 by Collins Crime

1 3 5 7 9 10 8 6 4 2

© Malcolm Forsythe 1996

The Author asserts the moral right to be
identified as the author of this work

A catalogue record for this book is
available from the British Library

ISBN 0 00 232594 2

Set in Meridien and Bodoni

Photoset by Rowland Phototypesetting Ltd
Bury St Edmunds, Suffolk
Printed and bound in Great Britain by
Caledonian International Book Manufacturing Ltd, Glasgow

All rights reserved. No part of this publication may be
reproduced, stored in a retrieval system, or transmitted,
in any form or by any means, electronic, mechanical,
photocopying, recording or otherwise, without the prior
permission of the publishers.

CHAPTER 1

On a warm June night, a woman in a white summer dress jumped out of a parked car in the lonely Essex countryside. Behind her as she walked away down the lane, she heard the car's engine start and the crunch of tyres as it began to move. Trudy Thornton continued walking, expecting the car to drive away in the opposite direction. Instead, she realized, it was coming along the lane towards her. As she turned, shielding her eyes against the glare of the headlights, the driver revved the engine and accelerated.

In sudden terror she looked around. The narrow lane had steep banks on either side with thick hawthorn hedges along the top. Dropping her handbag, Trudy kicked off her high heels and began running.

The headlight beams scythed the darkness in front of her and ahead she saw a break in the bank where there was a gateway into a field. She raced towards it and heard the car's engine rise to a crescendo. She started screaming.

The front bumper rammed her behind the knees and she was flung back against the bonnet and catapulted into the air. She landed head first then rolled over and over with the momentum and came to rest lying across the lane and unconscious.

The car stopped a few yards short of where she lay and stood with its engine ticking over. Then slowly, the driver steering carefully, it moved forward. The front wheel went over Trudy Thornton's neck, crushing her windpipe and snapping her spine. She died instantly.

The driver got out and dragged her body to the rear of the car then opened the boot and, lifting the body by the shoulders, tumbled it in. Closing the boot, the driver – a blurred figure in the red glow of the rear lights – turned and walked back along the lane to recover Trudy's handbag and shoes. These were tossed in on top of her body and, with a glance up and down the lane, the shadowy figure returned to the driver's seat and drove away.

Shortly after one o'clock in the morning, a container-lorry thundering northwards along the A12 rounded the bend at Feering. Its headlights picked out a white bundle in the middle of the road and a split second later the driver realized it was a woman in a white dress, and slammed on his brakes.

The articulated lorry jack-knifed and slewed across the road, its wheels aflame with burning rubber as it careered sideways over the tarmac towards the motionless figure lying in its path. The driver looked down helplessly from his cab, sobbing with fright as the woman's body was crushed beneath the wheels.

Detective Chief Inspector George Millson arrived late at his office. He'd spent half the morning interviewing four women who had replied to his advertisement in the local paper for a domestic help.

When Millson's thirteen-year-old daughter, Dena, had opted to live with him rather than her mother and stepfather, they had divided the household chores of the semi-detached house in Lexden between them. The arrangement had worked well but now, Dena having moved up a class at school, and having more homework, Millson decided the time had come to employ a cleaning-woman.

He found that interviewing prospective female employees was not at all the same as questioning witnesses and suspects. His formidable bulk and close-cropped dark hair did nothing to put them at ease. Moreover, he was on edge with them because he had given up smoking a week ago and was longing for a cigarette.

He should have gone to an agency, he thought, after the first interview, and certainly he should have worded the advertisement differently. He'd specified: 'cleaning-woman and general help'. Apparently, there were clear rules as to what cleaners did and did not do, and there were recognized hourly rates for them around Colchester. A general help was altogether different.

The first woman asked what he meant by 'general help'. When he told her he expected her to do the washing and ironing, she said, 'Certainly not! I don't do things like that.' She was outraged, as though he'd asked her to strip for him.

The second woman seemed old enough to be his grandmother and Millson doubted she could have carried the vacuum cleaner upstairs. The third applicant was a long-legged teenager with freckles who'd just left school. She told him she wanted temporary work while she looked around for a 'proper job', so he ruled her out.

The fourth and last candidate was a surprise, but just as unsuitable as the others, Millson decided, when he opened the door to her. She had short blonde hair, and wore a cream trouser suit. A black shoulder bag dangled at her side and the fingernails of her hand clutching the strap were painted a pearl colour. She didn't look as though she'd done a day's housework in her life.

'Mrs Victoria Gill?' he asked, recalling her typewritten application. She was the only one of the four who had offered references.

She stepped past him into the hall and gazed around like a prospective buyer. 'Ms,' she said cheerfully, pronouncing it 'murz'. 'I reverted to my own name after my divorce. Well, if he didn't want *me*, I certainly didn't want his *name*.' Her voice was firm and clear.

She asked crisply what hourly rate he was offering. Millson, who had been thinking in terms of a weekly wage, said it would depend on how much help she was prepared to give.

'I see.' Her plucked eyebrows lifted in twin arches no thicker than HB pencil lines. 'Perhaps you'd show me round then and point out what you'd like done.' Opening her bag, she took out a notebook and pen.

Millson took her round the house room by room, and as she made notes his confidence in her increased. They came to Dena's room . . . bed unmade . . . knickers and tights left lying on the floor.

7

'She doesn't have time to tidy her room before school,' he said apologetically.

Victoria Gill nodded sympathetically. 'No mother around to keep her in order?'

'No.' Millson didn't elaborate.

'I had the same problem with my son,' she said. 'He's left home now, thank goodness.'

'You don't look old enough to have a grown-up son,' Millson said.

She laughed. 'Thank you. I'm thirty-eight. I married young.'

In the kitchen she inspected the washing-machine and the dishwasher and nodded approvingly. 'Let's see then . . .' She studied her notes. 'Say six hours a week to keep the place clean and tidy and cope with the washing and ironing. For that' – she did a calculation in her notebook – 'we would charge . . .' She quoted a figure.

'We?' Millson queried.

She put the pen between her teeth, delved in her bag and handed him a card. VG CLEANING SERVICES, it read.

'VG stands for "Very Good" as well as being my initials,' she explained. Her blue eyes met his frankly. 'I'm sorry I misled you, but we badly need new business and it frightens domestic customers off if I write in on the firm's stationery. I have a staff of four.'

'So, you wouldn't be doing the work yourself?' He was disappointed. She'd been his last hope and he'd been impressed with her efficiency and businesslike attitude.

'Not normally. Is that a problem?'

'I'm a police officer. I can't have an assortment of strange women having the run of my house.'

'I'll do the job myself then,' she said promptly. She saw his lips purse. 'I'm not afraid to dirty my hands, you know. I stand in for my staff when they're away.' As he hesitated she went on, 'I'll throw in some gardening for free, if you like.' She pointed a painted fingernail at the wilderness on the other side of the kitchen window. 'My flat doesn't have a garden and I love gardening.'

'You're on,' Millson said. 'When can you start?'

'Hadn't you better take up my references first?'

He'd already checked the applicants' names against the National Criminal Record Index and local police records, and from her confident manner he thought it unlikely her references would be unfavourable. 'I'll take your word for them,' he said.

'OK, then.' She smiled. A feature he liked about Victoria Gill was that she smiled with her eyes as well as her mouth. She took an exercise book from her bag and turned the pages. The pages were divided into columns and ruled like a school timetable. 'I can do three hours on Mondays and Fridays, starting next Monday. Will that be all right?'

'Fine,' Millson said.

'I'll need a key, please.'

He nodded and went in search of a spare front-door key.

Millson had barely sat down at his desk when Detective Sergeant Scobie put his copper-coloured head round the door. Scobie was twenty-eight and ten years younger than Millson. He told Millson about the body that had been lying on the A12 in the early hours of the morning.

'It looks like a hit-and-run case,' he said. 'The victim is a Trudy Thornton, aged thirty-five. The lorry driver called the emergency services, but she was dead when the ambulance got there. The police doctor who attended reckoned from the body temperature that she was already dead when the lorry went over her. We've put out the usual roadside notices and media appeals for witnesses and information.'

'Where was this?' Millson asked.

'On the northbound carriageway of the A12, just past the slip road from Feering. She lived in Feering so she might have been taking a short cut across the A12 on foot,' Scobie said. 'It saves a long walk up a slip road, over a flyover and down the other side.'

'Uh-huh. Next of kin informed?'

'Yes . . . her mother lives in Sible Hedingham.'

Millson grunted. It seemed to be a straightforward hit-and-run case. Possibly the driver had panicked and would come forward voluntarily when his conscience began pricking him.

Or again he might not, when he heard the victim was dead. 'We're going to have a job tracing the driver if he doesn't come forward of his own accord,' he said.

'Could be a she,' Scobie said.

'The statistics are against you, Norris. Hit-and-run drivers who kill are almost invariably male.' He rose from his desk. 'We'd better have a word with the mother and see if she can throw any light on her daughter's movements last night.'

Crossing the car park to his car Millson asked, 'When's the postmortem?'

'Tomorrow afternoon at four.'

Millson opened the car door. 'It'll be routine. You go, Norris.'

'OK.' Scobie settled himself into the passenger seat. 'How did you get on with the chars this morning? Did you find one?'

'Yes, a rather superior one, and I don't think she'd like to be called a char. I'm hoping she'll be a good influence on Dena and persuade her to keep her room tidy.'

'Do you think Dena will wear that, George?'

Scobie had joined Millson three years ago when he transferred from the Metropolitan Police, and the comfortable relationship between them allowed him the occasional use of Millson's first name.

'I don't see why not. It's a fair exchange for not having to help with the housework,' Millson said, fastening his seat belt.

Scobie doubted if Millson's daughter would see it like that. She had been allowed her own way in the house for the past year and, from what he knew of Dena, she would resent the intrusion of another female.

Charles Howard too had arrived late at his office that morning, although not as late as Millson. He had spent last night at his flat in Pimlico. Normally, when he stayed in town, he walked to his office at Queen Anne's Gate. This morning, however, it had been raining and he had taken the Underground from Victoria. There had been one of those interminable delays – a breakdown of some kind further along the line – and he had been trapped between Westminster and St James's Park for over an hour.

Emerging from St James's Park station, he crossed the road to the tall building opposite and walked past the main entrance to another entrance further along that was reserved for senior staff. With a nod to the security guard, he inserted his pass into the security lock beside the narrow revolving glass door and keyed his personal code. The door swivelled open and when he stepped through, it shut behind him, enclosing him in a glass tube. The security guard at the desk pressed a button, releasing the inside half of the revolving door, and Charles Howard stepped out and walked to the lift beyond. Entering the lift, he pressed the only button and the lift began its ascent directly to the twelfth floor.

Charles Howard was an under secretary in the Police Department and was expecting to be made deputy secretary in charge of the department in the near future. He was forty-six, a tall man, with alert blue eyes and grey streaks in his dark hair. His goal, and expectation, was to become permanent secretary within five years. He'd graduated from Cambridge with a first in mathematics and natural philosophy and since two out of the last three permanent secretaries in the Home Office had been Cambridge men, Charles Howard considered this gave him the edge over the other candidates.

Reaching the twelfth floor he proceeded along the corridor to his office. As was customary on his first arrival, he entered via an outer office which housed his private secretary and two personal secretaries. At other times he used the door to his room further along the corridor, from which it was a short step to the permanent secretary's office next to the Home Secretary's suite at the end of the corridor.

With a brief 'Good morning!' he swept through the outer office and entered his room.

Roger North, his private secretary, jumped up from his desk and followed him in. Roger had joined the department straight from university and had been Charles Howard's private secretary for six months. He was twenty-four, but his golden curls and a habit of blushing made people think he was younger.

11

'The House sat late and I stayed in town last night,' Howard said. 'Then this morning there was a breakdown on the Underground.' He threw his briefcase on the desk in annoyance.

Roger nodded sympathetically. He was surprised Howard had decided to man the official box himself instead of leaving it to one of the principals in F1 division. An uncontested one-clause amendment hardly required an under secretary in attendance on the Minister. Closing the door, he cleared his throat.

Charles Howard looked round. 'Don't worry, Roger, I haven't forgotten Sir Robert's meeting at twelve.'

'It's not that, sir. There's been some bad news about Trudy . . . Miss Thornton.'

Howard paused in arranging papers on his desk. 'What sort of bad news?'

'I'm afraid she was killed in a road accident early this morning. Her mother telephoned Personnel a short while ago.'

Howard stood like a statue for several seconds. Then, 'How very sad,' he said and resumed arranging his papers.

Roger North stared at him. Was that all the man could say about the woman who had been his personal secretary for years?

Glancing up, Howard saw Roger's shocked face and added quickly, 'It's a tragedy and I shall miss her terribly. Draft me a letter of sympathy to her mother . . . and I shall attend the funeral, of course. Now' – he sat down at his desk – 'let's go through your note of the last ACPO meeting. Sir Robert will want to hear how it went.'

When the Hansard reports of yesterday's proceedings in the House arrived later, Roger North scanned them for items to be marked for his under secretary's attention. There were none. The amendment had been called at 10.15 and disposed of at 10.30. The adjournment debate that followed – and had gone on until after midnight – had been about farming subsidies. These were nothing to do with the Home Office and Roger wondered why Howard hadn't gone home after the amendment was passed. Why spend the night at his flat?

CHAPTER 2

Trudy's mother, Joyce Thornton, was in her late fifties, a plump woman with a rosy complexion and fair hair turning white. She had been roused from her bed in the early morning to identify her daughter's body in the mortuary, and her face was still haggard with shock when she opened the door of her bungalow to Millson and Scobie.

She took them into her front room and began battering Millson with questions, leaving him no time to answer. How had it happened? Had the lorry driver fallen asleep? What speed was he doing? Had they tested his brakes? Suddenly, her face crumpled and tears squeezed from under her lashes and ran down her cheeks.

Millson sat her down gently in an armchair and sent Scobie to the kitchen to make tea. Through her tears she said miserably, 'I try to be brave . . . but Trudy was all I had since her dad . . .' Her voice faltered. '. . . died two years ago. This would have broken his heart.' She took a breath. 'It was him shortened her name to Trudy, you know. She was christened Gertrude – after my mother – and when she was a little girl . . .'

Millson listened sympathetically to Mrs Thornton reminiscing about her daughter's childhood, closing his mind to her pain, until Scobie returned with three cups of tea. Then, sipping tea, he edged her towards the matter of her daughter's movements the previous night.

'Trudy had her own place in Feering, I gather, Mrs Thornton?'

'Yes, a nice little cottage. She bought it about eight years ago. She works in London, see, and it's handy for the station at Kelvedon.'

13

'It's quite a walk from Feering, though,' Scobie commented.

'Oh, Trudy used her bike – 'less it was raining. Then she took the bus.'

'We'd like to know how she came to be walking on the A12 last night,' Millson said. 'Is it possible she was taking a short cut across the road when she was knocked down? Perhaps returning from visiting friends on the other side of the A12?'

'No, there's nothing 'cept fields and farms over there,' Mrs Thornton said firmly. ''Sides, Trudy told me she'd be staying late for an office party yesterday evening.'

'I see,' Millson said. 'So, she would have travelled home by a late train?'

'Unless she had a lift home from the party and was dropped off by the slip road from Feering. It's only a short walk to her house from there. Maybe she was walking towards the slip road when the lorry hit her. He must've been drunk not to see her! Did they breathalyse him?' she demanded.

'It's routine after an accident,' Millson told her. 'But it wasn't the lorry driver's fault, Mrs Thornton. I don't think he had a chance. Your daughter had been knocked down earlier and was lying in the road. The police doctor thinks she was already dead when the lorry ran over her.'

'Oh.' She caught her breath in surprise. 'A hit-and-run, you mean? They didn't tell me that.'

'We shan't know for certain until the postmortem,' Scobie said.

She turned a tear-stained face to him. 'Postmortem? That means they'll cut her up, doesn't it?'

'Only if it's necessary to establish the cause of death,' he assured her. Trudy's death seemed a straightforward case. If there had been suspicious circumstances the pathologist would take her apart to check on everything from her last meal to her sex life, and then cobble the body together for the undertaker. Or sometimes, in a murder case, for a second examination by a pathologist hired by the defence.

Millson said, 'If Trudy *was* given a lift home, Mrs Thornton – all the way from London – it would be by someone who lived in this direction. Do you know who that might be?'

She pursed her lips. 'Her boss, maybe. He sometimes gives her a lift.'

'And who would he be?' Millson asked.

'Mr Charles Howard. Trudy was his secretary and he'd have been at the party, I expect. He's what they call a Whitehall mandarin – leastways, that's what Trudy called him.'

Scobie took out his notebook. 'Do you know his address, Mrs Thornton?'

'It's called The Lawns. It's on the Nayland Road as you get out of West Bergholt.'

As Scobie made a note Millson asked, 'Is there anyone else who might have given her a lift? A boyfriend, perhaps?'

Mrs Thornton shook her head. 'She don't have a regular boyfriend at the moment. Last time she was going with someone was over a year ago.'

Millson nodded and stood up. 'Thank you, Mrs Thornton. Is there anyone you'd like us to contact? Someone to come and sit with you?'

'No, I'll be all right, thanks.' She took out a handkerchief and wiped her eyes. 'You just find who killed my Trudy and put him away.'

'We'll do our best,' he promised.

'We'll go back via West Bergholt,' Millson said as he started the car. 'And see if this Charles Howard is at home.'

From the road, the entry to The Lawns was between two high hedges and opened on to an acre or so of smooth green grass. In the middle stood a Georgian house and as Millson drove towards it along the short drive, an elderly man on a motor-mower veered across the grass and took up a parallel course, waving at him.

Millson stopped and lowered his window. The man brought the mower to a halt and switched off the engine. 'Ain't no one in!' he called.

'When will they be back?' Millson asked.

'Mrs H in a coupla hours, Mr H about seven. 'Oo shall I say called?'

'Thanks. Don't bother,' Millson said.

*   *   *

15

Scobie watched apprehensively as the pathologist, David Duval, began the autopsy. He had attended postmortems before, but not with Duval and not one where the victim had such extensive injuries.

'Oh dear, oh dear,' said Duval, as he lifted the covering sheet from the corpse. 'What a mess.'

'She was run over by a ten-ton truck,' Scobie informed him.

'And looks like it,' said the pathologist.

As he worked, Duval dictated his notes into a tape recorder. After a while he laid down his instruments and stood back with a frown. 'We have something of a puzzle here, Sergeant,' he said. 'I shall need to go over my notes and do some more tests. What I can tell you at the moment is that the cause of death was a broken neck, and she died before incurring the further injuries from the lorry.'

'The police doctor told us that much,' Millson said irritably when Scobie reported to him later in the afternoon. 'What's his problem? She was killed by a hit-and-run driver and then run over by the truck, wasn't she?'

'I think it could be more complicated than that,' Scobie said. 'Duval gave me the impression some of the injuries occurred before her neck was broken.'

'Do you mean she'd been beaten up?' Millson demanded.

'I don't know,' Scobie said defensively. 'He's carrying out more tests.'

Millson snorted and looked at his watch. 'Well, we can't wait for Duval. Charles Howard should be home by now.'

The green front door of The Lawns was opened by a woman in a black cotton dress that fitted her like a sheath. She was very tall, with shoulder-length blonde hair and she loomed over Millson and Scobie like a Valkyrie selecting warriors for death as they stood a step below her at the door.

'Yes?' Her tone of voice implied they were tradesmen who should have used the back door. Or perhaps, Scobie thought, as she glanced at his business suit and briefcase, she believed

16

they were from a religious organization that was currently canvassing the area.

'We're police officers.' Millson showed his warrant card and introduced himself and Scobie. 'We'd like a word with Mr Howard if he's around, please.'

She was unimpressed. Policemen obviously ranked with plumbers and Jehovah's Witnesses. 'What about?' She slightly aspirated the H without sounding affected, Scobie noticed.

'I'll explain that to him myself if he's in,' Millson said, annoyed by her manner.

'Oh, very well.' Her eyes went beyond them to Millson's car. 'I hope your car doesn't leak oil,' she said. 'We've just had fresh gravel put down.' She had a clear, carrying voice, like a stage actress.

Millson had part-exchanged his elderly Ford Sierra for the nearly-new Rover less than a month ago and Scobie saw him struggling to keep his temper. 'It doesn't — and it had better not,' Millson growled.

'Good. Come this way then,' she said.

They followed her inside and across a square-shaped hall to one of the oak doors opening from it. 'Wait in here.' She ushered them through the door and closed it on them.

The room was a study-cum-library. The shelves of books with faded covers — among them Millson noticed *Halsbury's Laws of England* — and the well-worn arms of the leather armchairs either side of the Victorian 'Partners' desk, seemed to belong to a past era. The fax machine and answerphone on the table next to the desk, though, belonged very much to the present. A copy of that day's *Times* lay on the desk, folded in four to display the crossword. Millson glanced at it. The crossword had been completed in a bold hand without a single alteration.

The door opened and Charles Howard entered. He wore a dark-grey pinstripe suit and a tie Millson was unable to identify. His entry, his cadaverous face, and the sharp blue eyes that raked Millson and Scobie from head to foot, brought a change of atmosphere to the room. The high forehead and

17

hard, straight mouth indicated a man of intelligence, but a man without compassion.

'My wife informs me you're police officers. How may I help you?' His tone was polite but cool. 'Do sit down.' He waved at the armchairs and sat down at the desk.

Lowering himself into one of the brown leather armchairs, Millson said, 'We're making enquiries into the death of Miss Gertrude Thornton, Mr Howard.'

'Trudy. Yes. A dreadful thing to happen.'

'I understand she was your secretary.'

'Yes. She'd been with me ... oh ... twelve years, I suppose.'

'So, you knew her well.'

Charles Howard's surprisingly long eyelashes fluttered briefly. 'Officially ... yes. I knew very little of her private life.'

'Her mother told us you were at a party together last night.'

'Not together, Chief Inspector,' Howard said firmly. 'The Private Office – the Minister's Private Office, that is – held a party to which all the personal secretaries were invited ... mine included. I looked in on it as a matter of courtesy – as did several other AUSs.' He saw Millson's eyebrows lift. 'Assistant under secretaries,' he explained. 'So you see, we weren't together.'

Millson wondered why Howard felt it necessary to empha-size the point. 'Miss Thornton was run over by a lorry on the A12 near Feering,' he said, 'and we're anxious to discover how she came to be at that particular spot late at night. Her mother suggested she'd been given a lift home from the party and dropped there. Possibly by you, she thought.'

'Oh no, certainly not.' Howard looked pained. 'I can't imagine why Mrs Thornton should think that.'

'Because you've sometimes given Miss Thornton lifts in the past, I gather.'

'Well, yes, I have ... occasionally ... if I happened to be travelling by car. I rarely take the car to London, though, Chief Inspector. I usually drive to Colchester station and take the train.'

'And yesterday, sir?'

Scobie caught Millson's uncharacteristic 'sir' and wondered if he was deferring to Charles Howard because he was a top civil servant, or was about to be rude to him. You couldn't always tell with Millson.

Howard hesitated. 'I *did* have the car with me yesterday, as it happens, but I stayed in town last night. I have a small flat in Pimlico which I use when I'm kept late at the House.' He saw Millson's eyebrows rise again and added, 'The House of Commons.' He smiled thinly. 'For my sins, I sometimes have to sit in the official box to the right of the Speaker.'

'I see. Then do you know how Miss Thornton planned to travel home after the party?'

'I really have no idea, Chief Inspector.'

'Was there anyone at the party who might have given her a lift to Feering?'

'How on earth should I know?' Howard's voice sharpened.

'I just thought you might, sir, that's all.' Millson rose to his feet. 'Thank you, Mr Howard. We won't take up any more of your time.'

Driving along Bergholt Road, Millson said, 'He didn't seem very upset over his secretary's death, did he?'

'I don't suppose his sort have feelings,' Scobie said sourly. 'I'll bet he never bothered to remember her birthday or bought her a present.'

Millson glanced at him in surprise. 'What's got into you, Norris?'

'Postmortems don't usually upset me, but I can't forget her mangled body lying on the slab. That poor woman worked for him for years and he didn't even look sorry she was dead.'

Millson grinned. 'I didn't much care for him, either.' He glanced down at the fuel gauge. 'I need petrol.'

He pulled into the next filling station.

Duval phoned Millson the following afternoon. 'Sorry for the delay . . . I had problems sorting out the injuries. My report's being typed, but I expect you'd like a rundown of it now.'

'Yes, please.'

'Well, to start with, this woman has three quite separate lots of injuries.'

'You mean she was run over by *three* vehicles?' Millson asked incredulously.

'No, I'm saying she has been hit three *times* by a vehicle. That's not the same thing. The first set of injuries comprise bruises on the back of the legs, a fractured skull and grazes on the arms and face. These are consistent with being hit by a vehicle from behind, striking the road head first and slithering along the ground. In the second incident, which occurred soon after the first, she suffered fractured ankles, a crushed larynx and a broken neck. Again, consistent with being run over by a vehicle. That's when death occurred. Thirdly, there are multiple injuries – crushed thorax, broken arms and legs, internal damage – caused by the lorry running over her dead body.'

'And all these injuries were caused by vehicles?' Millson asked.

'In my opinion, yes.'

'No doubt about the broken neck?'

'No doubt at all. There's a tyre mark on her throat.'

'Had she been drinking?' Millson asked.

'Yes, but not heavily. She'd have been perfectly capable of walking straight and wouldn't have wandered about drunkenly in the road, if that's what you're thinking. And it wasn't just bad luck that the wheel went over her neck.'

'What do you mean?'

'There are no impact abrasions on the skin, so the wheel was moving very slowly.'

Millson sat up straight in his chair. 'Are you suggesting the vehicle was driven over her deliberately? That she was murdered?'

'That's how it looks to me.'

Millson heaved a sigh. A murder case just as he'd decided to give up smoking was something he could have done without. 'How long between the first and second lot of injuries?' he asked.

'I thought you'd ask that,' Duval said smugly. 'Not long.

Taking into account the bleeding time of the first batch of injuries, I'd say only a minute or so.'

'Could they have occurred at the same time? From the front and rear wheels passing over her in succession, perhaps?'

'Not a chance. The first injuries arose from being struck at speed and thrown into the air.'

Millson began doodling on the notepad on his desk. 'And how long had she been dead when the lorry ran over her?'

'Anything between half an hour and two hours.'

'Are you sure? Even at that time of night a dead woman couldn't lie on the A12 for long without being noticed,' Millson said.

'I haven't said she did,' Duval said. 'From the marks of oedema on the body I'd say life was extinct before it was laid in the road. So, after she was run over, she could have been carried to the side of the road, kept out of sight, and then placed in the road just before the lorry came along. But that's for you to establish, Chief Inspector. I can tell you, though, that my theory is not inconsistent with the medical evidence.'

'Thanks for your help,' Millson said drily.

'Oh, one other thing.' Duval's tone was casual.

Millson clamped his teeth together. Duval had an irritating habit of holding back a significant item until last. 'And what might that be?' he asked patiently.

'She was pregnant.'

'How long?'

'About two months.'

21

As Millson sat at his desk mulling over Duval's call, his hand strayed to his pocket for a cigarette. Then he remembered. Two days without a smoke and it seemed like eternity. He reached into his desk drawer and took a lump of barley sugar from the packet there and popped it in his mouth. Sucking its soothing sweetness, he swung his chair round and lifted a reference book from the shelf behind him.

A while later he banged on the partition wall to summon Scobie from next door. 'I've just had the path. report,' he said, when Scobie appeared. 'Trudy Thornton was pregnant and she was murdered. Knocked down and deliberately run over a second time to finish her off, and the body dumped on the A12 to make it look like a hit-and-run accident. Question is, was this a genuine accident where the driver panicked and ran over her again to prevent her identifying him? Or did he intend to murder her all along?'

'Must've been an accident to start with,' Scobie said. 'You wouldn't set out to murder someone that way.'

'Oh, it's been done before,' Millson said. 'Though apart from detective stories and gangster films, there's only one case where someone was convicted of using a car as a murder weapon.'

From the expression on his face, Scobie guessed Millson had already looked it up. Millson often used the criminal statistics and reports of previous cases to guide his choice of lines of enquiry.

'James Robertson, Glasgow 1950 . . . a serving police officer,' Millson went on. 'His mistress, Catherine McGluskey, had had a child by him. He knocked her on the head then ran his car backwards and forwards over her to make it look like a hit-and-run accident. Made a terrible mess of her in the process.'

'Like Trudy Thornton,' said Scobie, recalling her broken body as Duval peeled the sheet from it.

'That was done by the lorry,' Millson pointed out. 'Our killer finished his victim off neatly by driving a wheel over her neck.'

'But you reckon he was Trudy's lover, like the Glasgow case?'

'What I reckon at this stage, Norris, is that as she was pregnant, and forty-three per cent of female homicides are committed by a lover or spouse, he's definitely the man to investigate first.' Millson's eyes flicked briefly to the ceiling. 'I'll trot upstairs and let the superintendent know we're in business.' He stood up. 'Usual procedures, Norris. Incident room . . . appeals for information . . . and have her clothes sent to forensic. With luck, they'll give us a line on the killer and where the body was lying before it was put on the A12. And collect the accident-investigation team's photos and any of her belongings found at the scene.'

When Millson returned from briefing his superior, Scobie was examining the contents of Trudy Thornton's handbag. 'There's not much in her diary,' he said. 'Mostly routine appointments and one or two dates with a Roger and an Alec, whoever they might be.'

'One of them's probably the man friend.'

'Her mother said Trudy didn't have one.'

'Well, *we* know that she did,' Millson said. 'She couldn't have got pregnant by herself.' Scobie resisted the temptation to make a quip about artificial insemination and anonymous donors. Millson went on, 'We'd better let Mrs Thornton know her daughter was murdered before the media find out. And she can probably tell us who Roger and Alec are. Then we'll go to Feering and see where the body was planted. Bring the keys from her handbag. We'll have a look round her house at the same time.'

'Have you found the driver?' Mrs Thornton asked as they followed her into the front room and sat down.

'Not yet, I'm afraid,' Millson said. 'And we haven't been able to establish how Trudy travelled home from the party. Mr Howard didn't give her a lift – he stayed in town Wednesday night. Perhaps Trudy had a friend you didn't know about – someone she met recently. In the last six months, say.'

She shook her head. 'No. She'd have told me. Trudy always told me everything. Like I said, there was no man in her life at present.'

Millson's tone was kindly. 'There has to have been, Mrs Thornton. Trudy was two months pregnant.'

'Don't be ridiculous! 'Course she wasn't! Where'd you get that from?'

'The pathologist who conducted the postmortem.'

'Then he's made a mistake,' she said confidently. 'Trudy would have said. We didn't have secrets from each other, and she knew I'd have loved a grandchild.'

'I assure you there's no mistake.'

She stared at him suspiciously for a moment then shook her head in bewilderment. 'I can't understand it then.' Her voice changed. 'Why are you telling me this now she's dead? I'd rather not have known. What's it got to do with the accident?'

He said gently, 'Trudy's death wasn't an accident, Mrs Thornton. We think she was run down deliberately.'

'Oh, no!' Her hand flew to her mouth. 'I – I don't understand. Why would anyone do that to Trudy?'

'I don't know, but I intend to find out. To start with we need to establish Trudy's exact movements on Wednesday night, and who she was with. Can you tell us any more about the party she went to?'

Mrs Thornton shook her head. 'Only that it was in the office. Mr Howard could tell you more.'

Scobie asked, 'What was Mr Howard like as a boss, Mrs Thornton? Did he treat Trudy well?'

'Oh, yes. Very well. Bought her little presents and so on. She thought he was a wonderful man to work for.'

Frowning at Scobie's diversion, Millson went on, 'And we want to speak urgently to the man she was on intimate terms with – the man who made her pregnant. Can you help us there?'

'No, I've told you, Chief Inspector, she wasn't going with anyone. I'm certain she wasn't.'

Millson signalled to Scobie who unlatched his briefcase and took out the diary. Opening it, he said, 'Her diary shows what look to be appointments with someone called Alec, Mrs Thornton. Who would that be?'

'*Appointments* with Alec? Show me,' she demanded.

Glancing at Millson first for confirmation, Scobie handed it to her. Scanning the pages, she said dismissively, 'Oh, them. Them's not appointments, them's the times she booked his taxi for. She always booked Alec when she wanted a taxi – especially late at night. She said she felt safer with someone she knew.'

'How well did she know him?' Millson asked.

'Alec?' She wrinkled her forehead. 'She went out with him for a while, but it finished over a year ago. She was still friendly with him, though.'

Scobie took out his notebook. 'Can you give us his surname, please?'

'Pethard. He lives in Earls Colne.'

'She was also meeting someone called Roger,' Millson said. 'Who was he?'

'That'll be Roger North in her office,' said Mrs Thornton. 'Yes, they used to go to the theatre together. There was nothing in it. Trudy was just friends with him like she was with Alec.' She saw Millson looking doubtful and went on sharply, 'Trudy and me were close, Chief Inspector. She would have told me if she was sleeping with them.'

Millson nodded. 'We'll need to interview both men. Do you happen to know this Roger North's address?'

She shook her head. 'It's somewhere in London. Mr Howard would know. Roger worked for him.'

Millson stood up. 'Thank you, Mrs Thornton, you've been very helpful. Do you have a photograph of Trudy we could borrow, please?'

She put a hand to her face in alarm. 'Oh dear, I suppose it'll be in all the papers. It don't seem right . . . pictures of her in the papers . . . reporters . . . Oh dear,' she repeated. Rising to her feet she went to the sideboard and picked up a framed photograph. 'You'd better have this one,' she said, handing it to him.

The woman in the photograph had dark, bobbed hair, and a slightly sulky face with a sensuous mouth. She looked younger than thirty-five and Millson guessed it had been taken some time ago. 'Your daughter was very attractive,' he said, passing the picture to Scobie.

'Oh yes, Trudy had no problem pulling a man when she wanted to,' Mrs Thornton said with a note of pride. 'She just didn't seem to bother much.'

Or did she simply keep her mother in ignorance? Millson wondered.

'And we need to search Trudy's house,' he continued. 'Would you like to be present while we do that?'

'Oh no, I'd rather not,' she said anxiously. 'It'd upset me seeing you rummaging through her things. I know you have to – her being murdered and that – but I couldn't bear watching you turn her home inside out.' Her eyes glistened.

'We won't disturb it more than we have to,' Millson assured her.

From Sible Hedingham Millson chose a route to Feering that took them via Marks Tey and southwards along the A12. Taking the slip road to Feering that went over a flyover across the A12, he stopped on the flyover and gazed down at the bend in the dual carriageway below. On the far side of the flyover was the slip road to the northbound carriageway and, beyond it, the place where Trudy Thornton's body had lain.

'A driver coming round that bend in the dark wouldn't see a body in the road until it was too late to avoid it,' Millson commented. 'I'd say the spot was picked deliberately.'

He drove on across the flyover and down the slip road on the other side. Just before it joined the carriageway there was a lay-by for a bus stop. He parked his car in the lay-by and, followed by Scobie, stepped across the slip road and on to the grass verge of the A12. He stood well back from the edge as the Friday-evening traffic hurtled past along the dual carriageway.

'According to the photographs, the body was in the middle of the carriageway about there,' said Scobie, pointing.

Millson nodded, visualizing the scene late on Wednesday night with hardly any traffic about. He glanced back at his Rover in the lay-by. Trudy Thornton's killer had probably parked there too . . . with her body hidden in the boot of his car. He would make sure nothing was coming, quickly carry the body to the middle of the carriageway, then return to his car and drive out of the slip road on to the carriageway, and on towards Colchester. It would only take a moment. He raised his eyes from the lay-by. The nearest house was some distance away and screened by a high hedge.

'I think her killer knew the area,' he told Scobie.

'Charles Howard would know it,' Scobie said impishly. 'He brought her home sometimes.'

'I'll ignore that, Norris,' Millson said sourly, making towards his car. 'Let's get up to the house and find out who made her pregnant, and why he hasn't come forward. There must be a clue to who he is there somewhere.'

Trudy Thornton's house was the middle one of three small cottages that overlooked a green some two hundred yards from where the slip road joined the A12. The cottages had tiny front gardens and long, narrow ones behind with a right of way across them to provide access to the rear of the buildings.

Inside, Trudy Thornton's cottage was neat and tidy. Downstairs, an inglenook fireplace took up one side of the living-room and a narrow door led through to a small, newly fitted kitchen that looked out on to the back garden. Upstairs, there was a large bedroom and an equally large bathroom.

In an hour of searching, Millson and Scobie found no clue to the identity of Trudy's man friend. No letters, no photos . . . nothing. Everything pointed to the cottage being the home of a bachelor girl. Except the magazines. There were current issues of *Mother and Baby*, *Baby and You* and *Your Baby* on the bedside table.

'Well, one thing's for sure,' said Millson. 'She wasn't planning on having an abortion.'

'And loverboy killed her because he didn't want the baby, which is why he hasn't come forward as an innocent father-to-be would do. Maybe he's been here and cleared out the evidence about him,' Scobie suggested.

'Either that, or Trudy was unusually secretive,' said Millson. 'I can't believe there isn't a mention of him somewhere. Have a couple of WDCs search through Trudy's things – women are better at this than men. And while they're at it they can ask the neighbours about her visitors. Where's her bike, by the way?'

'It'd still be at Kelvedon station if she came home by car.'

'Probably. Although she may have taken the train and been knocked down cycling home from the station. I want it found and checked. And post a couple of uniformed men at the station with copies of her photo to ask passengers if they saw her on Wednesday night.'

Returning along the A12, Millson turned off it for Eight Ash Green and West Bergholt. 'We'll ask Howard about Roger North,' he said. 'And maybe he'll be more forthcoming about his secretary when I tell him she was murdered. He must know *something* about her private life after all the years she's been working for him.'

Charles Howard opened the door to them himself. He was wearing a dinner jacket and invited them in with barely concealed irritation. As they followed him across the hall to the study, Laura Howard came down the stairs. She wore a simple white evening gown with a one-shoulder cutaway that showed off her figure to perfection. She saw them and paused, one hand resting on the banister rails.

'Darling, don't be long,' she called. 'We mustn't be late, you know.'

Her husband nodded and ushered Millson and Scobie into the study. 'We're dining with the Lord Lieutenant,' he explained as they sat down. 'So I'd be glad if you'd be brief.'

'I'll do my best,' Millson said. 'So far, we haven't established how Miss Thornton travelled home Wednesday night, and we've been unable to trace her man friend.'

Howard looked down at his desk. 'Did she have one?'

'Oh yes,' said Millson, watching his face. 'According to the postmortem report she was two months pregnant.'

Howard's face stiffened, though Millson didn't think it was from surprise. 'How unfortunate . . . that an unborn child was killed as well, I mean.'

Scobie asked, 'You didn't know your secretary was pregnant?'

Charles Howard regarded him disdainfully for several seconds before answering. 'No, Sergeant, how should I?'

'I would have thought she'd have told you, or at least told other people in the office. Most women are pleased when they become pregnant and can't wait to tell everyone.'

'Do they? Really?' Howard's tone was bored. 'Did she tell her mother?'

'No, as a matter of fact, she didn't,' Scobie said.

'Which seems to refute your previous statement,' Howard said. 'Nor, so far as I am aware, did she tell anyone in my office.' He gave Scobie a wintry smile. 'I cannot answer for the rest of my department, of course.'

'Perhaps you can help us about her man friend, though,' Millson said. 'Her mother doesn't know who he is, so he could be someone she met at work. Was she particularly friendly with anyone there?'

'Not that I noticed,' Howard said curtly. 'I suggest you ask my private secretary, Roger North. He knew her quite well. And he arranged the party that evening, so he can probably tell you when she left and how she travelled home.'

Scobie took out his notebook. 'Where can we contact him, please?'

'He lives in Finchley, but I know he's spending the weekend down here in Tanniford, so you'll find him there tomorrow. He uses his parents' old house in Ferry Street as a weekend retreat. I imagine anyone in Tanniford could tell you the number.' He turned to Millson. 'I fail to see what all this has to do with your investigation of a hit-and-run accident, Chief Inspector.'

'It wasn't a hit-and-run accident, Mr Howard. Trudy was murdered. She was run down deliberately and her body placed on the A12 to be run over again by the next vehicle that came along,' Millson said.

'How do you know that? What's your evidence?' Howard demanded.

Millson bridled. 'That's not something I can discuss.' He had not told the press exactly how Trudy Thornton had been killed and he didn't intend to tell Charles Howard either.

Howard picked up a letter-opener from his desk and began tapping it against his hand. 'One of my responsibilities, Mr Millson, is to chair meetings of ACPO – the Association of Chief Police Officers. I know your Chief Constable extremely well.'

'Do you, sir? How interesting.' Millson had not intended to question Howard, but the reference to a cosiness with the Chief Constable needled him, and he decided he would. He went on, 'On the occasions you gave Miss Thornton a lift home, did you take her right to her door, or drop her off near the exit road to the A12?'

'What an extraordinary question,' Howard said.

'Do you mind answering it, please.'

'It so happens I've done both.'

Before Millson could frame his next question Scobie suddenly asked, 'Why did you take your car to London on Wednesday, Mr Howard?'

Howard seemed disconcerted by the question and took his time answering. 'I had a meeting at the staff college in Sunningdale that morning. It was simpler to drive across country in my own car, and then on to London, rather than take the train to town and use an official car from the office.'

Ignoring Millson's frown, Scobie pressed on. 'May I ask why you didn't drive home in it, then?'

Howard hesitated. 'I was late getting away from the House and I was tired. So . . . as I told you . . . I stayed in town.'

Millson gave a warning grunt to silence Scobie and asked, 'Would you mind telling us what time you left the House of Commons that night?'

'I don't remember exactly. But it was late, as I said.'

'There'd be some record of this, would there, sir?'

Charles Howard looked down his nose. 'I don't book in and out like a factory worker, Millson. I have a pass.' His voice trembled with anger.

Calling George Millson by his surname, without rank or title, had no more effect than a child banging its head against a brick wall, however, and Millson continued, unruffled, 'Someone would have seen you leave, surely?'

'I left by way of the members' exit to Westminster station and not through the main gate, so I very much doubt if the constable on duty noticed me.'

'And where did you go after that?' Millson asked.

'Oh, really!' The words exploded from Charles Howard's lips. 'What on earth have my movements to do with the death of my secretary?'

'I have to establish the whereabouts of everyone connected with the victim at the time of the murder,' Millson said, and couldn't resist adding, 'As my Chief Constable will confirm if you care to ask him, Mr Howard.'

Howard's face flushed with annoyance. 'I took the Underground to Victoria, walked to my flat and went to bed.'

'Is there someone who can vouch for that?'

'No, there is not!' Howard said tersely. He looked pointedly at his watch. 'Now, is that all?'

'Yes, thank you, and I hope you enjoy your dinner with the Lord Lieutenant,' Millson said, rising to his feet.

'Thank you,' Howard said curtly.

At home later that evening Millson's daughter asked, 'When's this cleaner-woman starting, Dad?'

'Monday,' he said.

'Oh, good. I don't need to do my room this weekend, then.'

'You most certainly do,' Millson said severely. 'She's coming to do the housework, not to clear up after you.'

Dena made a face. 'What's she like? Some old bag, I suppose.'

'She's smart and attractive and her name's Victoria.'

'How old is she?'

'Thirty-eight.'

'That's old,' said Dena.

'*I'm* thirty-eight,' he said.

'Yes, but you're my dad,' she said obscurely.

Alec Pethard sat in his cab in the taxi rank outside Colchester station listening to the midnight news on the local radio. The police were treating Trudy Thornton's death as murder, the newscaster said. Alec chewed his lip. Best to call in the police station first thing in the morning, he decided. It would look suspicious if he waited for them to come to him.

CHAPTER 4

On Saturday morning Millson drove directly from his home to Tanniford to pick up Scobie and interview Roger North. Last summer, Scobie had moved in with his girlfriend, Kathy Benson, who managed the estate agent's there and lived in the flat above.

The village of Tanniford lay in a bend in the Colne. There was no bridge across the river and the only way into and out of the village was over the bridge across the railway cutting at the top of the High Street. The estate agent's stood on the corner of the High Street and Station Road, and as Millson drove over the bridge and parked outside it, Scobie came out of the door to greet him.

''Morning, sir. Ferry Street starts just opposite. North's place is halfway down on the right.'

Ferry Street was a narrow street without pavements and with barely room for two cars to pass. Fifty yards along, it turned at right angles and ran down across East Street and on past the Black Dog to the quay. The houses had been built as fishermen's cottages in the late eighteen hundreds, and the front doors opened directly into the street. Outside Roger North's house a bronze Saab 900 convertible was parked close against the front window.

Roger North opened the door to them wearing a short-sleeved check shirt and blue jeans. He showed no surprise when they identified themselves. Millson asked if he'd been forewarned of their visit by Charles Howard.

'Actually, it was Mrs Howard who phoned me,' North said, looking embarrassed. 'Do come in.'

The front door led straight into a large downstairs area that had been created by removing the hallway and the dividing walls between the rooms. At the rear there was a kitchen and a small enclosed backyard. Stairs in the far corner of the room led to the upper rooms, and in the alcove beneath was a dining recess with pine table and chairs.

Roger North had visitors. They were sitting on the sofa under the front window. Turning his head to glance at them, Scobie was suddenly transfixed. Although he'd heard of Tanniford's Habenhowe twins from Kathy Benson, he'd never seen them and he was taken aback – not only by their total identicalness, which was remarkable enough – but by their startling beauty, which Kathy hadn't mentioned. Their perfect features and unblemished complexions were the stuff of fashion and beauty magazines. One girl looking like that would have attracted Scobie's attention, but *two* . . . exactly alike . . . side by side . . . heads tilted at the same angle . . . legs crossed the same way . . . He was riveted.

They were young; he guessed them to be no more than a year or two past twenty. Their straight, chestnut-coloured hair – darker than his own – was cut in a short pageboy and shone like burnished copper. Looking down on their heads, he could see the identical whorls at the crown – a characteristic of monozygotic twins, like their identical genes, blood group and fingerprints.

Their eyes, cornflower-blue like their summer dresses, gazed up at him, unsmiling, showing no response to his open-mouthed admiration. Feeling foolish he turned away, realizing they must be used to being stared at. He glanced at Millson to see his reaction to them and was piqued that he seemed unmoved. To his disappointment, Roger North didn't introduce the twins but told them abruptly, 'You must leave now. These police officers want to ask me about an accident to someone in my office.'

They remained seated, regarding him with unwinking eyes.

'Please.' There was a note of desperation in his voice. 'I – I'll see you in the Dog this evening.'

They nodded and, in perfect accord, uncrossed their legs and rose to their feet. Moving to the door they stood waiting. Roger North hurried forward to open it for them.

'Bye, Biggy,' they said in unison as they went out.

Closing the door, he said offhandedly, 'They're the Haben-howe twins – Georgina and Georgette.'

Scobie ran his eye over North who was of medium height and slim. 'Biggy?' he queried.

'It's a nickname they once gave me.' Roger North blushed furiously at the memory of his boyhood experiences at the hands of the Habenhowe twins.

In the street outside, the engine of the Saab turbo revved loudly, the noise echoing between the houses as it shot away.

'I wonder they can get insurance to drive a car like that at their age,' Millson said.

'Georgina and Georgette can get anything,' Roger North said sourly, seating himself on the sofa they had just vacated. 'What did you want to ask me, Chief Inspector?'

Millson settled into a button-back armchair. 'Tell us about the party Trudy went to last Wednesday. You organized it, I believe.'

'Yes. It was nothing spectacular, just a drinks-and-nibbles affair paid for out of the Perm Sec's hospitality fund. It was to show the department's appreciation of the extra hours the staff of the Private offices put in on the Police Bill.'

'Who was at the party?'

'Personal secretaries . . . staff from the various Private offices . . . and a few typists.'

'Was Trudy with anyone in particular that evening?'

'It wasn't that sort of party, Chief Inspector. People merely chatted and circulated.'

'I understand Mr Howard was there for a while.'

'Yes, he looked in on his way to the House.'

'What time did Trudy leave?'

'About half-ten, I think.'

'Alone?'

'Yes.'

'Do you know where she was going?'

'To Liverpool Street, I assume, to catch her train home.'

'She was quite attractive,' Millson said. 'Did she have a boyfriend in the office?'

'Not to my knowledge.' North smiled. 'She used to say she was in love with her job and Charles Howard.' He saw

Millson's expression change and hastily added, 'She was only joking, Chief Inspector – about Mr Howard, I mean.'

Millson shifted in his chair. 'Weren't you a boyfriend? You had dates with Trudy . . . lots of them. She wrote them down in her diary.'

Roger North blinked and said quickly, almost gabbling, 'Yes, but they were just shows I took her to . . . and sometimes we had dinner afterwards. She had no one to go with, you see, and we both liked opera and the theatre.' He took a breath and went on, 'It was convenient . . . for both of us. It's not much fun going to a show on your own.'

'What was your relationship with her?'

'We were just good friends.' North gave a shaky laugh. 'I know that's a cliché, but it's true.'

'How good? Were you intimate with her?'

Roger North's eyes opened wide. 'Look here . . . I had nothing to do with her being pregnant!'

'Answer the question, please. Did you have sex with her?'

'No.' North lowered his eyes.

Millson studied him, trying to discern if he was lying. Did North go for older women? Trudy Thornton must have been at least ten years his senior. 'Did she tell you she was pregnant?'

'No. I had no idea until Mrs Howard told me last night.'

'Were there any rumours about her in the office?'

'Not that I heard.' North appeared to relax and become more sure of himself. 'Rumours in Private offices are mainly about Ministers, Chief Inspector. And their wives and girlfriends – or boyfriends, as the case may be. Not about staff. No one's interested in us.'

Millson grunted and nodded to Scobie to take up the questioning.

Scobie began, 'Trudy was Mr Howard's personal secretary and you're his private secretary. What's the difference?'

North smiled disparagingly. 'Rank, for a start. I'm a principal. My job is to carry out research and prepare briefs for Mr Howard, and draft answers to PQs – parliamentary questions.'

'You don't actually perform any private duties for him?'

36

'If you mean concerning personal matters, no. That's what a personal secretary is for. That was Trudy's job.'

'Seems a bit of a misnomer to call you a private secretary, then,' Scobie said.

'We're all secretaries of one sort or another in the administrative class, Sergeant, and the higher the rank the more humble it sounds,' North said, appearing aggrieved. 'The grade above me is an assistant secretary. After that comes assistant under secretary, deputy under secretary and finally permanent under secretary – the head of the department.'

'So, Mr Howard is only two from the top,' Scobie commented. 'He must be a pretty big fish.'

'That's one way of putting it, I suppose,' Roger North said disdainfully.

Scobie opened his notebook. 'Did Trudy ever mention a man called Alec? Alec Pethard?'

'Yes. Her friendly taxi driver, she called him. She used to phone him to meet her at Colchester station if we were late coming out of the theatre and she'd missed her train to Kelvedon.'

'Do you know if she asked him to meet her on the night of the party?'

'I'm afraid I don't.'

'What time did *you* leave the party?'

'I stayed to the end.'

'And then what?'

North hesitated. 'I – um . . . went to Liverpool Street and took a train to Tanniford.'

Millson suddenly raised his hand at Scobie and leaned forward. 'You came down *here* that night, Mr North? Why?'

'To get the place ready for the weekend . . . air the beds . . . turn on the fridge and so on.' North looked uncomfortable.

'What time train did you catch?'

'The two minutes past twelve.'

Scobie, who'd resumed writing when Millson took up the questioning, looked up sharply. He and Kathy sometimes caught a late train home after an evening in London. 'The last train to Tanniford is the nine minutes past eleven, Mr

North. The two minutes past twelve only goes as far as Col-chester.'

Roger North looked confused. 'Oh . . . well . . . I didn't mean I caught a train right to Tanniford. As you say, that train ends at Colchester. I took a taxi from there to Tanniford. It only takes about fifteen minutes,' he ended lamely.

Millson regarded him keenly. The man looked worried. Because of his slip over the trains? Or was it something else?

'Is there someone who can confirm your movements that evening after you left the party?' he asked.

North gazed at him as though mesmerized. 'Er . . . no. No, there isn't.'

'He's lying,' Millson told Scobie as they walked back to Kathy Benson's. 'He's lying about the trains and he's lying about why he came here that night. Airing the beds! In *June*? Find out what time his train arrived in Colchester and have some-one check with the station taxi rank to see if he took a taxi to Tanniford as he says.'

Through the window as they neared the estate agent's, Millson saw Kathy Benson's auburn head bent over her desk. 'What about inviting me in for coffee, Norris?' he asked. 'Then I can say hello to Kathy.'

'You mean pump her about Roger North, don't you?'

Millson grinned. 'Why not? She knows everyone in the village. She's lived here all her life.'

So too had Roger North until he was eighteen and went to university, Kathy told Millson. He'd lived in the house in Ferry Street with his parents. After university he'd joined the civil service and gone to live in London. Then six months ago, when his parents retired to the south coast and made over the house in Ferry Street to him, he'd started spending his weekends there.

'He's a bright cookie, though a bit immature,' Kathy said. 'And squeaky-clean. Even the Habenhowe twins couldn't bed him.'

'They were at his house this morning,' Scobie said. 'I don't see why he doesn't jump at the chance to take one of them out. They're very attractive.'

'They're also very weird,' Kathy said. 'They never go any-where without each other so you can't take out one twin, you have to take them both. And it's a mind-blowing experi-ence, I'm told.'

Millson asked, 'Does Roger North bring a girlfriend here on his weekends, Kathy?'

'The word is there's one around. I haven't seen her, though,' she said.

He took Trudy Thornton's photo from his pocket and showed it to her. 'What about this woman?'

Kathy shook her head. 'I haven't seen her here.'

Millson had finished his coffee and was saying goodbye to Kathy when the phone rang. Scobie answered. It was a DC in the incident room. Alec Pethard had walked into Colchester police station and asked to see the officer in charge of the Trudy Thornton murder case. Should he interview him? the DC wanted to know, or ask him to wait for DS Scobie or Mr Millson.

'Tell them to hold on to him until we get there,' Millson said when Scobie asked him.

Pethard was a tall, lanky man of about thirty-five in wire-rimmed spectacles. His hair was dark and curly and he wore a black leather jacket.

'I heard about the murder on the radio last night,' he explained as he seated himself in Millson's office. He spoke in a hoarse voice like someone with a sore throat. 'They said anyone who'd had contact with her recently should come forward. Well, I have, and I didn't want you calling at the house and upsetting the missus, so I've called in.'

'Go on.'

'Well, there's not much to tell. She always used to book me when she wanted a taxi because she knew me. We'd been out together a few times in the past, see?'

'How did you meet Trudy?'

'She hired me taxi, didn't she? A right looker, she was . . . an' I fancied her like mad. Me wife had just walked out on

me, see? I turned on the old charm . . . chatted her up . . .
an' got lucky.'

'You had sex with her?'

There was a barely perceptible pause before Pethard said,
'No, we didn't get that far.'

'When was this?' Millson asked.

'A couple of years ago. We broke it off a year back when
the wife walked back in again.'

'Was that at Trudy's request or yours?'

'It was mutual.'

'So, what sort of terms were you on after that?'

'Friendly, that's all. Trude phoned me sometimes when
she wanted a cab.'

'Quite a few times, according to her diary,' Scobie said.

'Yeah, well, she felt safe with someone she knew, see?
'Sides, I gave her cheap rates . . . for old times' sake.'

'Did she phone you last Wednesday night?'

'No.'

'For the record, Mr Pethard, where were you between
eleven-thirty and twelve-thirty that night?'

'Out Tiptree way. I picked up a fare from the Mercury at
eleven,' Pethard said promptly, indicating he'd prepared his
answer beforehand.

'Tiptree is not far from Feering,' Scobie commented.

'Nor are most of the places I take fares to from Colchester,'
Pethard said.

'The point is, you were in the vicinity when the victim
met her death,' Millson told him.

'So were a lot of other taxi drivers at that time of night, I
expect,' Pethard said.

'But they haven't had an association with the dead
woman,' Millson pointed out.

'An' that's why I come forward, isn't it?' Pethard said.
'Soon as I heard the appeal on the radio.'

'Or was it because you knew we'd find your name in her
diary?' Millson asked, and saw Pethard's eyes flinch. 'Where
did you go after you'd dropped your fare?'

'I was finished for the night. I went home to Earls Colne.'

'What time did you get there?'

"Bout half-one, I suppose.'
'Anyone to confirm that?'
'No, the wife was in bed asleep.'
'Did you know Trudy was pregnant?' Millson asked.
'Not till I heard on the radio.'
'Anything else you can tell us?'
'No. I've done my duty and that's it.'
'Well, thank you for coming in, Mr Pethard,' Millson said.
'We may need to speak to you again.'
'Sure. Any time,' Pethard said confidently.

At midday, as Alec Pethard's red Mercedes rejoined the line
of waiting taxis at Colchester station, a dark-blue Mondeo
coasted down the hill into Tanniford, turned into East Street
and drove into the car park at the rear of the Black Dog.

Laura Howard swung her long legs from the driving seat
and stood up. Lifting a hamper from the passenger seat, she
locked the car and walked up Ferry Street. She tapped lightly
on the door of Roger North's house and slipped inside as he
opened it.

'Charles thinks I'm shopping in Colchester,' she said with
a gurgling laugh. 'We can have the whole afternoon. I've
brought lunch and a bottle of bubbly.'

She set the hamper down and put her arms around his
neck, pushing against him with her body. 'Darling . . . oh,
darling . . .' She seized his shirt-front and tugged him
towards the stairs.

CHAPTER 5

Laura Howard's affair with Roger North had begun six months ago, soon after he became her husband's private secretary. Charles Howard had been in Paris attending a European conference on border controls. Trudy Thornton, who was accompanying him, telephoned Roger with instructions to extract some statistics from a file in Howard's safe at his home, and fax them to her immediately as they were needed for a speech he was making the following day.

Roger had taken the next train to Colchester and arrived at West Bergholt in the late afternoon. He explained his mission to Laura Howard and she showed him to the safe in the study. The combination was the same as the one he was used to on the security cupboard in Howard's office, and he had the classified file out of the safe in a matter of moments. He turned with it in his hand and found Laura standing behind him.

'I could have done this for Charles if he'd given me the combination,' she said.

'I'm afraid that would be against the rules, Mrs Howard,' Roger said awkwardly.

'Oh dear,' she drawled, 'you're one of those boring men who worry about rules.'

He said nothing, feeling foolish as he tucked the file under his arm to hide the title on the cover. He'd only been in the job a few weeks and he didn't want to offend Charles Howard's wife. However, he'd already broken one rule in opening a security safe under the eyes of someone who didn't have access to it, and he didn't intend to make another slip. Closing the safe door, he spun the dial to scramble the tumblers, and moved to the fax machine beside the telephone.

'I do have to be alone while I do this, Mrs Howard,' he said apologetically.

'Of course,' she said mockingly. 'I shall tell Charles what a paragon of virtue he has in his new private secretary.' She turned and left the room, closing the door behind her.

He opened the file and copied out the figures Howard had asked for. Switching on the fax machine, he faxed the figures to the secretariat in Paris and returned the file to the safe. When he emerged from the study she was waiting in the hall.

In his haste he hadn't given her a second look before. She was dressed in black pantaloons and a white satin blouse, and as she stood by the hall window with the evening sun turning her luxurious blonde hair to gold, he realized she was strikingly attractive.

'I promise I didn't peep through the keyhole,' she said with a mocking smile. She saw him appraising her and her smile softened. 'You'll stay to dinner, of course,' she said. 'I'm sure Charles would want me to feed you and, anyway, I hate eating alone.'

He'd skipped lunch in order to catch the next train and he was hungry. 'I'd love to, thank you,' he said.

'Good.'

She led him into the spacious sitting-room. A grand piano graced the far end of the room beneath the high windows. Laura Howard waved her hand at the decanters and glasses on a sideboard. 'Help yourself to an apéritif while I rustle up a meal. There's a rather nice vintage sherry there.' The smile was slightly mocking again. 'And for goodness sake relax, Roger. You've done your duty.' She withdrew to the kitchen.

Roger North went to the sideboard. He didn't know how to tell which of the decanters held the vintage sherry, so he poured a glass from the lightest-coloured one and sat down nervously in one of the vast armchairs near the piano. He was awed by his hostess. She was taller than him, and the way she spoke to him made him feel like a small boy.

In the kitchen, Laura Howard prepared the starters. She heaped cream cheese on to slithers of smoked salmon, rolled them up, and added a lettuce leaf. For the main course, she put chicken breasts stuffed with garlic in the microwave and set a saucepan of rice to boil on the ceramic hob. As she lifted a bottle of wine from the wine rack and placed it on the worktop she paused and gazed out of the window into the gathering twilight.

She was forty, and she had been married to Charles Howard for eight years. She had selected him for her husband the same way she selected her career: by considering the options and going for the best one, regardless of obstacles – the obstacle in the case of Charles Howard being that he was already married.

At university she had taken a degree in fine art and then joined the staff of a women's fashion magazine. By the time she met Charles Howard she was its art editor and contemplating her next major decision: marriage. Laura was glamorous and intelligent and there was no shortage of suitors. She had narrowed the field to two: a merchant banker and a professor of history, when the magazine's editor inveigled her into attending an exhibition of prisoners' art at the Home Office.

'What for?' Laura asked suspiciously.

'They want someone to judge it and choose the three best pictures.'

'I can't judge pictures,' she protested.

'Of course you can! You took history of art, didn't you? Anyway, I've promised them you'll do it.'

Charles Howard had recently been promoted to under secretary and was standing in for the Director of Prison Services who'd been suspended from duty following a spate of prison break-outs. Laura was introduced to him at the preview and he accompanied her as she made a preliminary circuit of the exhibits. Laura was relieved to discover her task would not be as difficult as she had thought. Only a handful of the pictures merited a second look.

On her second round she paused at a canvas covered with frenzied daubs of red and black. Its implicit violence was frightening. Over her shoulder Charles Howard murmured, 'I wonder what this man is in for.'

'Serial murder and rape, I should think,' she said.

44

'Really? Can you tell from that?' He moved beside her and peered closely at the picture.

She laughed. 'No, of course not!'

Afterwards he invited her to lunch and took her to his club in St James's. Over martinis he explained why the department had not offered payment for her services. 'Wretched Treasury rules,' he said apologetically.

'Is that why you're giving me lunch?' she asked waspishly.

'No, of course not.' He sounded annoyed. 'I asked you to lunch because I find you extremely attractive.' She raised an eyebrow at him and he went on forcefully, 'Will you come to the opera with me this evening and have dinner afterwards?'

She gaped at him. It wasn't often a man took her breath away. 'You're a *very* fast worker, Mr Howard,' she said archly.

'Charles,' he said. 'Yes or no?'

Clearly, Charles Howard was not the stuffy civil servant she'd taken him for. However, Laura was not used to her escort galloping ahead like this and she sought to rein him in and regain the initiative. 'Yes . . . Charles . . . provided it's the Royal Opera at Covent Garden.' That would put him back in his box, she thought. At this short notice it was bound to be Sadler's Wells or the Coliseum.

'Well, of course it is,' he said with a touch of irritation.

'You can get tickets for this evening at the Garden just like that?' she asked incredulously.

His eyes crinkled at the corners. 'A colleague of mine has permanent use of a box there.'

'Oh,' she said, stunned. She recovered herself. 'Thank you. I'd be delighted.'

After an enjoyable evening, at the end of which he insisted on seeing her again, Laura made some discreet enquiries about him. She discovered that Charles Howard, then aged thirty-nine, had a brilliant career in front of him, would almost certainly rise to the top in the civil service, and was likely to collect a knighthood along the way. The discovery caused her to rethink her options for marriage. She had been hovering between the university professor, who was delightfully romantic, and the merchant banker, with the banker having the edge because of his wealth. Now there was a third option and it carried the prospect of a title. Lady Howard. That would be wonderful ... irresistible, in fact, Laura decided.

There was, of course, the problem that Charles Howard was already married. However, he didn't strike Laura as the faithful type, so she didn't regard that as much of an obstacle. It had been obvious from their first evening together that he was panting to get her into bed, and after a few more evenings she obliged.

Charles Howard was captivated by the glamorous Laura, and three months later she manoeuvred him into a divorce – not that he voiced any objection. They were married in the spring. The following summer, when she accompanied him to the Palace garden party for the first time, Laura was satisfied she had made the right choice.

The bell rang on the microwave and she turned from the window with a sigh. The problem now was that after eight years of marriage she was bored and in need of stimulation. And this was the fourth time in recent months that Charles had been away for several days attending a conference.

She went into the dining-room and began laying the table, her thoughts turning to Charles's new private secretary and his refreshing youthfulness. He was so earnest ... so serious. He positively invited teasing. It would be fun to tease him some more. Her evening could be quite amusing.

'Would you mind opening the wine, Roger?' she asked as they sat down to the meal.

He nodded and approached the bottle on the sideboard with trepidation. The double-action opener lying beside it was a type he hadn't used before. He didn't screw down far enough and as he wrestled with the levers the cork broke in half and came out on the end of the corkscrew. He stared at it in consternation, blushing furiously.

Laura rose from the table and took the opener from him. She became aware of his warmth and odour as he perspired with embarrassment. 'Do you always get hot and bothered when you do something wrong, Roger?' she asked teasingly.

'Er – yes, I suppose I do.'

With deft fingers she removed the cork debris, reinserted

46

the corkscrew and retrieved the remains of the cork from the bottle without crumbling it.

'There, that wasn't so bad, was it?' She patted his shoulder and handed him the bottle. 'Now you can pour.'

During the meal she quizzed him about his flat, and what he did in his spare time. He didn't have any with this job, he told her ruefully.

'Girlfriends?' she asked lightly.

He shook his head.

'You're not gay, are you, Roger?' she asked in mock horror.

'Good Lord, no!'

She laughed at his vehemence. 'I was only teasing. Do you like music?'

'Yes,' he said sulkily, annoyed by her teasing.

'Then I shall play for you,' she said.

After the meal, as he reclined in an armchair with the large brandy she had dispensed, she sat down at the piano and began playing. His annoyance vanished with the opening bars of a Chopin waltz. She was an accomplished pianist. He took a mouthful of brandy, mesmerized by the power of her performance . . . the swift fingers striking the keys . . . golden hair swaying with the movement of her arms. Another waltz followed and then the mood changed as she began a nocturne. He lay back and closed his eyes, letting the music wash over him.

Sometime later, after the haunting chords of *Tristesse* died away, he realized she had stopped playing and opened his eyes. She was standing looking down at him.

He scrambled to his feet. 'That was wonderful,' he said. 'Absolutely wonderful.'

She smiled at his enthusiasm. 'Thank you. Do I get a kiss for entertaining you, then?' she asked softly.

Self-consciously, he raised his face to kiss her cheek. She put her arms round his neck, cupped his head in her hands and redirected his mouth to hers. Her tongue forced his lips apart and slithered inside.

Ten minutes later he was lying naked beneath her on a bed upstairs.

47

CHAPTER 6

On Monday morning Millson received the report on the forensic examination of Trudy Thornton's clothes. There were
dark-blue fibres adhering to the skirt and bodice of her white
dress, indicating she had lain full-length on carpeting of some
kind. Microscopic examination revealed them to have simi-
larities with a nylon material commonly used to line car
boots. The dust and grit on her clothes could have come from
almost anywhere, but John Croft, the forensic scientist who
had made the report, suggested the impact debris, if it could
be found, would locate the scene of the crime.

'What the hell is impact debris?' Millson muttered, lifting
the phone and dialling Croft's number.

'Accident-investigation teams use it as a guide to speeds
on impact,' Croft explained. 'When a car hits an obstacle –
including the human body – the force of the collision dis-
lodges mud and debris from the underside of the vehicle. If
you look under your car you'll be surprised how much gunk
and grime you've picked up from the road. This woman was
hit hard and there is bound to be impact debris on the ground
where she was knocked down. This only happened a day or
two ago so it's probably still there. Find it, and you've found
the scene of crime.'

'That would be fine if we knew where to start looking. She
could have been killed anywhere between here and London,'
Millson said grumpily. 'Is this all you have? No paint fragments? No clue to the vehicle involved?'

'Afraid not.'

Millson grunted with frustration and replaced the phone.
Nothing had come of contacting the names and addresses in
Trudy Thornton's address book, and three days of appeals in
the media and questioning passengers at Kelvedon station

had brought no sighting of her on Wednesday night. Roger North had said she left the party to catch her train from Liverpool Street, but there had been no confirmation of that, nor of her arrival at Kelvedon. Kelvedon station was small and unmanned at night so she might not have been seen, but her bike had been found in the rack there and that suggested she had not reached the station that night.

He lifted the next paper from his in-tray. It was the report of the WDCs who had searched Trudy Thornton's house and questioned her neighbours. Although they had found a letter from a health clinic giving the date of her pregnancy test and confirming the result as positive, they had found no trace of the man she was involved with. However, they had obtained useful information from an old lady living next door. She told them she was often awakened by the noise of a diesel taxi bringing Trudy home late at night. Always the same taxi and the same driver, she said. Sometimes he accompanied Trudy into the house. Then later she would be woken again by the engine starting up when he left.

'Mind you,' she told them with a sniff, 'he didn't stay all night like he used to last summer.'

Had she heard the taxi last Wednesday night? No, she hadn't.

'Because he didn't take her home that night,' Millson muttered. 'Because . . . maybe . . . he took her somewhere else and killed her.'

He stood up from his desk and went into Scobie's room next door. 'Have Pethard brought in, Norris. He lied to us. There was more than friendship between him and Trudy. He was having regular sex with her.'

After an early start from Tanniford that morning, Roger North was far from alert as he tried to concentrate on what the junior Minister was saying. He was apparently expressing doubts about the proposal to pay prison officers by computer like the rest of the department's staff. It seemed he feared the prison officers might object to the idea and call a strike.

'He's being a wimp,' Howard said out of the side of his mouth to Roger.

49

Roger lowered his eyes. Sitting so close to the man whose wife he'd been in bed with all Saturday afternoon unnerved him. He began to sweat, worrying that Howard might suspect – perhaps catch a whiff of her perfume on his clothes, or read the guilt in his face.

Roger's previous sexual encounters had been with girls at university. His first time with the mature and experienced Laura, when Howard was in Paris, had been a revelation to him. Afterwards, he'd been overwhelmed with guilt. Yet when she telephoned the next time Howard was away and invited him to the house, he was on the next train. And from then on, whenever Howard went off to a conference, Roger went to bed with his wife.

Laura made his position clear from the start. 'I adore you, poppet, and you're gorgeous in bed, but I've no intention of taking risks with my marriage. If Charles becomes even the teeniest bit suspicious we're having an affair, I'll snuff it out like a candle. It would be over. Never happened. Understood?'

Roger's attention returned to the meeting as he became aware that Howard had intervened in the discussion. With cool politeness Howard acknowledged the Minister's concerns. He then proceeded to demolish them, excising each in turn like a surgeon with a scalpel and leaving the Minister no escape from deciding in favour of the proposal.

As the Minister began vacillating his anxious PPS leaned forward and breathed in his ear. The Minister nodded and rose to his feet to announce he was due in the House and would defer a decision until the next meeting.

Howard, angered by the delaying tactic, strode off to see the permanent secretary. Roger returned to his office to dictate a note to the agency girl who was temporarily covering Trudy's duties.

While she was typing it, his thoughts switched to Saturday again. Not to the afternoon with Laura, but to the evening with the Habenhowe twins in the Black Dog. There had been no threats, no hostility, and their faces were serene as they told him what they knew.

'Don't worry, we'll keep your secret, Biggy,' they'd said.

Through the window Roger gazed across the rooftops at the Scotland Yard building. There would be a price to pay for their silence, he was sure of that. There always had been.

Shortly before Alec Pethard arrived at the police station on Monday afternoon, a woman called there and said Trudy Thornton had travelled on her train Wednesday night and left the train at Kelvedon. She was interviewed by Scobie.

'It was the two minutes past eleven from Liverpool Street,' she told him. 'It arrived at Kelvedon just after midnight and she was the only person who got off there. She walked off the platform into the road and as the train pulled out I saw her getting into a car.'

'You're quite sure it was Trudy Thornton you saw?'

'Oh yes. I catch the ten to eight from Colchester every morning and I often saw her getting on at Kelvedon.'

'Can you describe the car?'

She shook her head. 'I'm sorry. It was dark and the reflections in the train window made it difficult to see clearly.' She wrinkled her brow. 'I think it was quite a big car.'

'Did she get into the front of the car or the back?' Scobie asked.

'The front, next to the driver.'

Scobie thanked the woman for her help, wrote out a brief statement for her to sign and took it to Millson. He was reading it when the front office rang to tell him Pethard had arrived and was in the interview room.

'Did he come in his car?' Millson asked.

'Yes, sir, a red Mercedes. It's outside in the car park.'

Millson put down the phone and finished reading. He looked up at Scobie. 'Trudy Thornton wouldn't have got into a stranger's car at that time of night, Norris. She must have known the driver. And Alec Pethard was in the area at the time. Let's take a look at his car before we interview him.'

Pethard's Mercedes had a dent in the front offside wing, and the colour of the interior furnishing was blue. Scobie was for taking fibre and hair samples from the upholstery.

Millson shook his head. 'There's no point. We know she

was a regular passenger in the car. You can ask him about the dent, though.'

Alec Pethard had come to the police station without protest, but when Millson switched on the recording equipment and cautioned him, he asked angrily, 'What's all this? I'm not under arrest, am I?'

'No, you're not, Mr Pethard,' Millson assured him. 'This is a standard procedure to protect your rights under the Police and Criminal Evidence Act.'

Pethard looked unconvinced. Adjusting his spectacles, he regarded Millson with suspicion. 'What d'you want me for?'

'I'd like you to answer a few questions,' Millson said. 'Tell me, how often did Trudy use your taxi?'

'Once or twice a week, I reckon.'

'Over what period?'

'About two years.'

'So, altogether she spent a good many hours with you in your taxi.'

'Yeah, I suppose so.'

'You must have learned a lot about her?'

The suspicion returned to Pethard's eyes. 'Not really. Very close, was Trude. She wasn't one for talking about herself.'

'What did she talk about, then?' Millson asked.

'Her evening out, usually. Whether she'd liked the film . . . concert . . . or whatever.'

'In all that time, did she mention another man?'

Pethard's eyes narrowed at Millson's use of 'another'. 'Yeah, sure she did. A guy called Roger. He's the one who took her to everything.'

'Let's stay with you, Mr Pethard,' Millson said. 'You told us on Saturday your affair with the dead woman was platonic.'

'What's platonic?'

'No sex,' Scobie told him.

Pethard ran a hand through his dark hair. 'Yeah, that's right.'

'You didn't ever spend the night with her?' Millson asked.

'No.'

'You see, a neighbour of hers says you did. Several times last summer.'

Behind the lenses, Pethard's eyelids flickered. 'That was a year ago, after the wife had left me. I've admitted I was going with Trude then. Yeah. I stayed the night a couple of times. I was upset and didn't want to go back to an empty house, so Trude let me sleep on her sofa.'

'And are you telling me you didn't have sex?'

'That's right.'

'I don't believe you,' Millson said.

'Well, I can't help that, can I?' Pethard said aggressively.

'All right, let's come to the present. This same neighbour says you often stayed for half an hour after you'd brought Trudy home at night.'

'Yeah, having a cup of tea.'

'A cup of tea,' Millson said with emphasis. 'You can afford to spend half an hour off the road at that time of night for a cup of tea, can you? I thought that's when business was brisk and taxi drivers made their money.'

'I only stopped if things were slack.'

'Uh-huh.' Millson nodded at Scobie to continue the questioning.

'There's a dent in the front wing of your car,' Scobie said. 'How did that happen?'

Pethard shrugged. 'Turning in someone's driveway. I nudged the gatepost.'

'When?'

'Weeks ago.'

'I don't think so,' Scobie said firmly. 'The metal underneath where the cellulose has cracked shows no sign of weathering.'

'OK, so it wasn't that long ago. Who cares?'

'We do, if it was caused by knocking someone down,' Scobie told him.

'I haven't knocked anyone down!' Pethard said.

Millson took over the questioning again. 'Where did Trudy usually ask to be picked up?'

'Kelvedon station, if it was raining and she didn't want to

bike. And Colchester station if she'd missed the last stopping train to Kelvedon.'

'When she hadn't booked in advance, how did she contact you?'

'On me mobile number.'

'Did she phone you Wednesday night?'

'No.'

'Did she usually sit in the front of your car or the back?'

'The front. Why?'

'A witness saw her getting into the front of a car outside Kelvedon station just after midnight on Wednesday. A big car, she thinks.'

'Well, it wasn't mine! I've told you . . . she didn't book me that night. And like I said before, I was taking a fare to Tiptree.'

Scobie said, 'You could still have got to Kelvedon station by eleven-thirty.'

'Why would I do that if she hadn't booked me?'

'Perhaps to take her somewhere and talk,' Scobie suggested.

'What about?' Pethard looked from Scobie to Millson. 'What about?' he repeated to Millson.

'What you planned to do about the baby,' Millson said.

'It wasn't me made her pregnant!'

'Then maybe you were jealous of the man who did and wanted to have it out with her,' Scobie suggested.

Pethard glared at him. 'How could I if I didn't know she was pregnant?'

'You could still have quarrelled over her going out with him.'

Pethard's voice rose. 'I didn't meet her Wednesday and we didn't quarrel over another man! That guy Roger's the one was screwing her, not me,' he said angrily. 'They were always out together. He's the one you want to talk to.'

'We have,' Millson said. 'He says he and Trudy were just good friends.'

'Well, he would, wouldn't he? He's lying!' Pethard shouted. He looked round wildly. 'I'm not answering no more questions without a solicitor.'

54

With no evidence on which to hold him, Millson said reluctantly, 'No further questions for the moment, Mr Pethard. You're free to go.'

Pethard scrambled to his feet, looking surprised and relieved as he hurried from the room.

'D'you think he was telling the truth?' Scobie asked Millson.

'No. At least, not when he said he didn't have sex with her. I'm not sure about the rest. But if *he* didn't pick her up from Kelvedon station on Wednesday night then someone else did. We'll put out an appeal for the driver. And now we know the time she left the station we may be able to find where she was killed.'

'How?'

'By finding the impact debris which forensic tell me is dislodged from the underside of the vehicle when it collides with something. Trudy was picked up at midnight and the pathologist estimated she'd been dead at least half an hour when the lorry ran over her. So, she must have been murdered between midnight and about a quarter to one.'

'You can drive a long way in three-quarters of an hour,' Scobie said.

Millson clicked his tongue impatiently. 'This man didn't take her for a romantic drive in the country, Norris. He took her to the nearest convenient place and killed her.' He glanced out of the window. 'It's too late to start now, but I want a search mounted in Feering first thing tomorrow morning. We'll cover the area within a mile radius of Kelvedon station to start with. The murder spot is likely to be somewhere quiet . . . away from habitation . . . so we'll concentrate on the lanes and byways.'

When he arrived home that evening Millson knew from his daughter's face she was in a bad mood. Her expression reminded him of his ex-wife, Jean, who used to bang things about and glower at him without speaking. Unlike her mother, Dena didn't remain silent for long before telling him the cause of her ill-temper.

She had come home from school early and found Victoria

55

Gill in her room. The room had not only been tidied but rearranged as well, and Dena was upset. Millson gathered there had been words.

'She had no right to turn my room upside down!' Dena stormed. 'My room's private. Tell her to keep out.'

He was about to come down heavily, and tell her it was her own fault for leaving her room in such a state, when he saw the tears gathering in her eyes. Dena had a right to be sensitive about her privacy, he supposed.

'All right,' he said. 'I'll ask her to leave your room in future, but you must do something for me in return.'

'What's that?'

'Put your clothes away and keep the room tidy.'

She sniffed. 'OK. Can I lock my door the days she comes?'

It wasn't worth arguing over. 'If you want to.'

Later, during their evening meal, she asked, 'What d'you know about Victoria Gill, Dad? Did you ask her for references?'

'Yes, and she supplied them.'

'Did you take them up?'

'No, but I checked that she doesn't have a criminal record.'

Dena sighed. 'Oh well, that's something, I suppose.'

The undertone in his daughter's voice had Millson wondering what had been said in the row between her and Victoria Gill. Wondering too whether he should have taken up the references after all.

CHAPTER 7

The next morning, for no reason he could think of, George Millson found himself plagued by a greater longing than usual for a cigarette. He supposed he'd reached a critical period of the withdrawal phase. Either that or it was because he'd slept badly due to churning the interview with Alec Pethard around in his mind. How could one prove a man had had sex with a woman at a particular time . . . like two months ago? In this case, that would be – That was when, sitting at his desk, Millson's thought processes veered off at a tangent.

If Trudy was two months pregnant the intercourse that led to it must have occurred sometime in April. Was it possible to narrow the period down? To a particular week, say? Even particular days, perhaps? If so . . . Another door opened in Millson's mind. Establish which man was with her at that time and – just as important – eliminate the men who weren't – and bingo! he'd identified his prime suspect. Millson firmly believed that, as in the Scottish case he'd cited to Scobie, Trudy had been killed by the man who'd made her pregnant.

How exact could one be, though? What he needed was more precise information than Duval had given in the post-mortem report – which simply said she was about two months pregnant. Millson picked up the phone.

'I'm a pathologist not an obstetrician!' Duval snapped when Millson put his question. 'I'll arrange for a colleague to examine the body.'

A Dr Taylor phoned Millson after lunch. 'I've examined the foetus, Chief Inspector. Why on earth do you want to know its age?'

'To establish limits for the date of intercourse, Doctor. That will enable me to concentrate on the men who had contact with her in that period and eliminate those who didn't.'

'Ah, I see. Well, I can help you there. It's possible to date a foetus fairly accurately by its stage of development. In this case it was just over eight and a half weeks old. When did the woman die?'

'Shortly before one o'clock in the morning last Thursday.'

'Let's have a look at the calendar. Thursday was the fifteenth of June so' – there was a rustling of paper at the other end of the line – 'intercourse and conception must have occurred between the fourteenth and eighteenth of April. There's the slight chance of delay between intercourse and fertilization, so you'd better work on thirteenth to eighteenth inclusive.'

'Thank you, Doctor. That's very helpful indeed.'

Millson put down the phone and went along the corridor to the incident room. Scobie had just finished briefing a team to search the Feering area for the murder scene. As the room emptied, Millson explained his idea to him.

'Bit of a long shot, isn't it?' Scobie said.

'We'll see. Dig out her diary and let's have a look at what she was doing between the thirteenth and eighteenth of April.'

Scobie retrieved the diary from the cupboard where the exhibits were stored, and turned the pages. 'On the thirteenth she had a hair appointment in her lunch hour and went to the theatre in the evening with Roger North. After that she seems to have been at home from the fourteenth to the seventeenth. It was the Easter holiday. Then on the eighteenth she went out with Roger North again. To a film this time.'

'Any indication of what she did over Easter?'

'Looks as though she was having some building work done. She's written: "FW fitting new kitchen".'

'Who's FW, I wonder?' Millson asked.

'The builder, probably. I'll see if he's listed in her address book.' Scobie went to the cupboard again and returned with the address book. He ran his finger down the index and flicked open the page. 'Here we are: Frank Worseley. There's a telephone number, and an address in Tanniford.'

Millson rubbed his chin, considering. 'Pay him a call, Norris. See if he can tell you what she was doing over Easter . . . who called . . . if she went out and so on. She was with North the day before and the day after Easter. Maybe he spent Easter with her as well.'

'You've gone off Pethard then?'

'He isn't mentioned on any of those dates.'

'She didn't always book him in advance. He told us so himself.'

'What's the matter with you, Norris?'

'Roger North doesn't look like a killer.'

'As I've said before, Norris, murderers seldom do. Now get off and see what you can find out from Mr Worseley. I'll be at Feering if you want me.'

It took Scobie the best part of an hour to locate Frank Worseley, and another hour to get there. His answering machine had given the number of his mobile phone, but there was no reply from it the first few times Scobie rang. Eventually Worseley answered and said he was working at an address in Mistley.

He was not doing much building work when Scobie arrived at the bungalow overlooking the Stour. He was sitting on the back step drinking tea and chatting to a woman in the kitchen. Worseley was in his late twenties with dark hair tied at the back in a ponytail, and his only clothing was a pair of faded blue shorts held up by a cord round the waist. His muscular torso was deeply tanned and his chest had a covering of dark hair that continued down over the abdomen into his shorts.

When Scobie introduced himself and showed his warrant card, Worseley put down his cup and got quickly to his feet. 'Shan't be a tick, missus,' he called out over his shoulder.

'Not here,' he muttered to Scobie, walking round to the side of the bungalow and beckoning him to follow. 'It's bad for business having police call on me.' He continued walking until they were at the front gate. 'OK. What's this about?'

'You did some work at Easter for a Miss Thornton in Feer-ing. Fitting a kitchen, I believe.'

Worseley scratched his chest. 'Yeah, what of it?'

'You know she was murdered?'

'Yeah, I seen it in the papers.'

'Can you give me the dates and times you were at her house, please?' Scobie took out his notebook.

'Whaffor? I got nothing to do with her murder.'

'We want to know what she was doing over the Easter period, that's all. You may be able to help.'

'Oh . . . well . . .' Worseley screwed up his face. 'I started work on the Friday morning . . . rippin' out the old kitchen an' that. Picked up the new fridge, cooker an' the rest of the stuff on Saturday, an' worked on till Monday night fixing it and fitting the worktop. Right sweat it was, getting it done in four days.'

'You were there every day?'

'Yeah, till eight or nine at night.'

'Did Miss Thornton go out at all over Easter?'

'No, she were there all the time.'

'Did anyone call?'

'Her mum were there Friday an' a coupla girls came on Saturday.'

'So the only man she saw over the whole of Easter was you?'

Worseley's eyes suddenly narrowed. 'Whatdya mean by that?' he asked suspiciously.

Scobie said patiently, 'We need to know whether or not she had any male visitors.'

Worseley smiled crookedly. 'Loverboys, you mean. No, I didn't see none.'

'Thank you, Mr Worseley. That's very helpful.' Scobie pocketed his notebook and turned to go.

'Ain't you found a boyfriend then?' Worseley asked.

Scobie turned back. 'Maybe . . . maybe not. Why do you ask?'

Worseley shrugged. 'Jus' interested.'

Scobie returned to Colchester and found Millson already

back from Feering. The search had not been successful and Millson had extended it to cover a two-mile circle from Trudy's house. As he listened to Scobie's account of his interview with Frank Worseley, a satisfied expression spread across Millson's face.

'This puts Roger North well and truly in the frame as her lover,' he said. 'If Worseley was working there until eight or nine every evening, as he says, and we rely on the evidence of Trudy's diary, then North is the only man who had access to her during the conception period.'

'Apart from the builder,' Scobie commented.

Millson sighed. 'Yes, all right, apart from the builder. Did anything come of the enquiries for the taxi North says he took to Tanniford Wednesday night?'

Scobie shook his head.

'So, let's assume he was lying about a taxi and wasn't on that train . . . didn't catch a train at all, in fact. And that's why he slipped up over the train times.' Millson stood up and went to the map on his wall. 'If he went down by car, Norris, how long d'you reckon it would take him to reach Kelvedon from central London?'

Scobie joined him at the map. 'I'd say about an hour at that time of night.'

Millson nodded. 'That's what I reckon. Which means he could have left the party after Trudy, as he says, and driven to Kelvedon station in time to intercept her as she got off her train just after midnight. After he killed her and dumped her body on the A12 he could have driven on to Tanniford, or back to London, and no one would have been any the wiser.'

'I don't see his motive,' Scobie said.

'He's a bright young man with a brilliant career ahead of him and he didn't want to be tied to a baby and a secretary who was ten years older than him.'

'Yes, but there are better solutions to that than murder,' Scobie protested.

'Norris, there are nearly always better solutions to a problem than murder. The point is, murderers don't choose them. If they did, there wouldn't be so many murders. Perhaps she was pressuring him into marriage by threatening to ruin his career. It wouldn't have done his promotion prospects much good if the top brass in the Home Office learned he'd put Charles Howard's secretary in the family way. They're a bit sniffy about that sort of thing, I imagine. North had a motive all right. I want him in for questioning.'

Roger North's hand was shaking when he put down the phone after Scobie's call. He'd agreed to drop in at Colchester police station on his way to Tanniford that evening. He hadn't intended going to Tanniford again until the weekend, but the police weren't prepared to wait until then. He knew why they wanted to speak to him and he didn't know how he was going to answer their questions. If only he hadn't made that stupid mistake over the trains.

He glanced across the room. Trudy Thornton's successor had her headphones on transcribing audio tapes and the door to Charles Howard's room was open which meant he was out.

He lifted the phone.

The search for the place where Trudy was run down ended in the late afternoon about a mile from her home in Feering. When Millson reached the little-used lane in open country, John Croft and a photographer were already there. In the gloom between the steep banks bordering the narrow lane, Millson peered sceptically at the small mounds that had been flattened by a passing vehicle.

'That's it?' he asked Croft, who was stooping to examine one.

'Yep. This is your murder scene,' Croft declared. 'This is where he ran into her.'

'It looks like mud to me.'

'No, this is not your ordinary mud,' Croft said, taking a pinch between finger and thumb and coming to his feet. He spread the substance on his palm and showed it to Millson. 'It's compacted dust – fortunately it hasn't rained since Wednesday – and it's black and oily. Ever noticed the grass verges of busy main roads? They're stained black with exhaust emissions and diesel fuel. I'll analyse a sample in the lab, but I can tell you now it's typical of the debris dislodged from the underside of a colliding vehicle.'

'OK,' Millson said. 'What else can you tell me?'

Croft pointed to the ground. 'There's only one area of debris, so this wasn't a collision between two vehicles. Now, I don't see any obstacle like a tree trunk or a lump of concrete lying around, so the collision must have been with a person or a large animal, and there aren't any cattle around here.' He walked a few paces in each direction. 'There are no skid marks, so the driver didn't apply his brakes before the impact.' He smiled confidently at Millson. 'Putting it all together, Chief Inspector, I'm pretty sure this is where your victim was run down.'

Millson nodded and looked up and down the lane. There was no ditch, and for some fifty yards in either direction the steep banks were topped by an impenetrable hawthorn hedge. This section of the lane was a death trap for someone trying to escape a pursuing car. He visualized the scene. Trudy leaving the car for some reason. Perhaps there had been a quarrel and she'd decided to walk home – her house was within walking distance. The car had followed . . . stalking her. She'd become aware of it and started running, but she couldn't outrun the car. The driver had aimed straight at her – there were no swerve or skid marks – and knocked her flying. Then, as she lay stunned and injured, he'd cold-bloodedly driven the wheel over her neck to kill her. Afterwards, he'd put her body in the boot, driven to the A12, and callously dumped it on the dual carriageway.

Moodily, Millson surveyed the steep banks and dense hedges. She'd been trapped . . . hunted down and destroyed like an animal. A vicious, merciless killing.

Roger North looked nervous in the interview room as Scobie switched on the recording equipment and Millson went through the formalities before taping the proceedings.

Millson began the questioning by following up Roger North's mistake over the trains. 'When we spoke to you before, Mr North, you told us you caught the two minutes past twelve train from Liverpool Street to Tanniford last Wednesday. Then, when Sergeant Scobie pointed out that that train ended at Colchester, you corrected yourself and said you took a taxi from Colchester to Tanniford. Do I have that right?'

Roger North cleared his throat. 'I didn't correct myself. I cleared up a misunderstanding over what I meant.'

'Uh-huh. Well, so there's no further misunderstanding, are you affirming you *did* catch that train and then hired a taxi at Colchester station to take you to Tanniford?'

'Yes.'

'Then we have a problem, Mr North. We've checked with the station, and that train arrived at twenty past one. But despite extensive enquiries, my detectives have been unable to find any taxi driver who took a fare to Tanniford off that train. Are you quite sure that was the train you caught?'

Roger North's eyelids fluttered. 'Yes. It's the last train.'

Millson nodded. 'We know. So why can't we find your taxi driver?'

'I don't know.' Roger North wrinkled his forehead and looked earnest. 'Perhaps he wasn't a regular taxi. There are some pirate ones around, I believe. Maybe that's the explanation.'

Millson turned a sceptical face to Scobie, who leaned forward and asked, 'Are you suggesting this was an illegal operator, Mr North? Not authorized to ply for hire?'

'Well, yes. Come to think of it, he didn't seem very professional. I mean, there's no way of telling, is there?'

'Yes,' Scobie said. 'Authorized taxis carry a council licence plate on the rear of the vehicle.'

'I didn't see the back of the car.' North sounded confident.

'What sort of car was it?'

'A Ford Sierra . . . black, I think, or dark blue.'

'And the driver?' Scobie snapped. 'Describe the driver.'

Roger North half closed his eyes as though in thought. 'I didn't see him very well in the dark. But he had a slight accent – could have been Asian.'

Scobie raised his eyebrows in incredulity and sat back in

his chair. Millson, using silence to underline his doubt, gazed steadily at North without speaking.

After a while, as North stared stolidly in front of him, Millson suddenly said harshly, 'You told us you'd never had sex with her.'

Startled, North said, 'Yes, that's right.'

Millson took Trudy Thornton's diary from the folder in front of him and opened it. 'According to this, you've been going out together regularly for months.'

'Yes, well, I've already explained that. She didn't like going to the theatre alone, and I was happy to escort her.'

Millson's tone changed, became friendly. 'Let me tell you what my difficulty is then. Trudy was two months pregnant . . . you're the only man she's been with . . . and you say you didn't have sex.'

'Oh, I can't believe I was the only man she went out with, Chief Inspector.'

'You certainly were between the thirteenth and eighteenth of April.'

Roger North stared at him blankly.

'You see,' Millson went on, 'the intercourse that led to her pregnancy took place between those dates.' He turned the pages of the diary. 'And I see that she was out with you on both the thirteenth and the eighteenth.'

The blank look vanished from North's face. 'Yes, but what about the other days?' He reeled them off: 'Fourteenth, fifteenth, sixteenth and seventeenth. She obviously had sex with someone then.'

Millson made a pretence of scrutinizing the days in the diary. He looked up. 'She didn't have any dates on those days,' he said.

'That doesn't prove she didn't meet someone,' North said positively. 'On her way to work . . . on the way home . . . in the evening.' Recklessly, he went on, 'And who knows what she got up to in her lunch hours? Trudy was always taking long lunch hours when Charles was out of the office. She had plenty of opportunities to get up to mischief in those four days.'

'Not really,' Millson said quietly, and sprang the trap. 'It was Easter and she was at home.'

Roger North's mouth dropped and his eyes opened wide. *Gobsmacked*, Millson thought, recalling his daughter's favourite expression. Relentlessly, he went on, 'Her mother came Good Friday, two girlfriends called on Saturday, and a witness confirms they were her only visitors over Easter.'

As Roger North sat trancelike, seemingly lost for words, Millson said coaxingly, 'Why don't you tell us the truth, Mr North?'

North came to life again. 'I have! I didn't have sex with Trudy! And even if I did, why should I kill her?'

'Perhaps you didn't want to have to marry a woman ten years older than you. Because that's what she'd expect you to do.'

'Look, I wasn't anywhere near Trudy's place that night. I was in Tanniford . . . miles away.'

'Do you own a car?'

'Ye-es.'

'Then I suggest what happened is this. On Wednesday you left the party after Trudy as you said. But you didn't catch a train. You drove to Kelvedon in your car and intercepted her at the station as she stepped off her train. You intended to reason with her . . . persuade her to have an abortion, perhaps . . . so you drove to a quiet lane to talk. But she wouldn't listen and you quarrelled. She jumped out of the car to walk home and you drove after her. Perhaps you didn't mean to run her over, but you did and then you panicked. Was that what happened? An accident?' Millson asked encouragingly, believing from North's expression he was near to confessing.

'No,' North muttered, and shook his head vigorously as though to clear his thoughts. 'No!' he repeated desperately. 'It's all wrong. Everything you've said.'

'Everything?' Millson asked mildly. 'Surely not. Some of it is established fact.'

'I didn't mean literally.'

'Tell me where I'm wrong, then,' Millson suggested.

'I didn't drive. I came down by train, as I said.'

'Ah yes,' Millson said. 'You caught a train to Tanniford that didn't go to Tanniford and you hired a taxi at Colchester that *you* can't identify and *we* can't find. And you can't produce a single witness to support any of this.'

Roger North clasped his hands together and stared down at the table. He hadn't thought it would come to this. He'd expected them to accept the story of a pirate taxi driver. There was nothing else for it now. He looked up.

'I *can* produce witnesses,' he said. 'The Habenhowe twins. I spent the night with them.'

CHAPTER 8

The Habenhowe twins were born in Tanniford in one of the weatherboard houses in West Street. Their mother worked in the local greengrocer's and their father was a deckhand on one of the fishing trawlers that operated out of Tanniford. Gladys Habenhowe insisted on giving birth at home, and the midwife who attended her maintained later that the doctor who delivered them discovered something special about the twins soon after they were born.

She'd sent for Dr Oakleigh when Gladys went into labour because, with Gladys being past normal child-bearing age, she feared complications. There weren't any, and as she watched the doctor examine the afterbirth – to show she understood what he was doing – she said, 'There's only one placenta, isn't there, Doctor? So, they're not fraternal twins. They're identical, aren't they?'

He nodded, preoccupied with his examination of the amniochorion. 'Yes, they're monozygotic. But there's more to it than that with these two. The wonder is they weren't born conjoined.'

'Siamese twins, you mean?'

Dr Oakleigh nodded. 'I think they separated very late.'

At the christening ceremony three weeks later, Gladys asked the vicar to christen the infants together. 'You mean literally at the same moment, Mrs Habenhowe?' he asked.

'Yes, please, Vicar.' She handed him the twins wrapped together in one bundle. To his relief they were no heavier than a single baby.

Standing at the font, out of habit he began, 'I name this child . . .' then corrected himself, '*these children . . .*' He scooped up a handful of water and paused, looking anxiously at Gladys.

She stared back blankly until, realizing he didn't know which was which, she reached out and pulled the shawl aside to reveal the labels she'd tied round their necks.

The vicar smiled and nodded. 'I baptize *thee* Georgina and *thee* Georgette,' he intoned, sprinkling water on the heads in accordance with their labels. Then, making the sign of the cross on each forehead, he continued, 'In the name of the Father and of the Son and of the Holy Ghost. Amen.'

The douche of cold water startled the twins. Two mouths opened, four lungs filled with air, and their howls of protest echoed around the church. Some of the villagers said in later years they'd always known the Habenhowe twins had the Devil in them from the way they screamed when the vicar marked them with the cross.

Dr Oakleigh had no such fancies about Georgina and Georgette, but he did offer Gladys some advice on rearing them the next time she visited his surgery. He urged her to treat them as individuals, and to encourage differences between them as they grew up. In particular, he warned her against emphasizing their likeness to each other. And, knowing her to be a stubborn and rather simple woman, he intended to reiterate the advice to her husband, Harry, when he next returned to port. The doctor never had the opportunity, though, because Harry Habenhowe was on his last voyage. The following night, as the trawler hauled her nets in rough seas off Bawdsey, a rogue wave washed Harry overboard and he was drowned.

Beyond her grief, Gladys discerned the hand of fate in Harry's death. A balancing of the scales. Fate had given her two wonderful babies and taken away her husband so that she could give them her undivided love and attention. And that is what she would do, she decided.

She was delighted with her two little look-alikes and, ignoring Dr Oakleigh's advice, she treated them like toy dolls, dressing them identically and reinforcing their sameness in every way possible. When, eventually, she realized her mistake, it was too late to rectify it.

The first hint of trouble came when Georgina and Georgette started to talk. Gladys feared they were backward because they spoke gibberish to each other and seemed incapable of learning words like other children. Then after a while it dawned on her that they were developing a vocabulary of their own, and could speak normally when they chose. She tried to stop them making sounds she didn't understand, but they simply spoke normally in front of her and reverted to their private language behind her back.

Gladys wasn't too concerned until, on the day of their seventh birthday, they started calling each other 'Georgie'. That was when she first became afraid the day was coming when she wouldn't know one from the other. It came sooner than she expected.

At the beginning she had guarded against mixing them up by attaching labels to their wrists and sewing name-tags into their clothes. Later, she put coloured bangles on their wrists – black for Georgina, red for Georgette. Then, when they were older and could read, she had their names engraved on bracelets which she made them wear at all times: at home, at school, in bed . . . in the bath. Especially in the bath. And it was at bathtime, when they were nine years old, that Gladys's fears were realized.

She had left them playing in the bath while she went to the airing cupboard for their clean clothes. When she returned, the bracelets were on the floor and Georgina and Georgette were sitting in the bath, giggling.

'Put your bracelets on at once!' Gladys ordered. 'You know you must never take them off.'

Sulkily, they clambered out of the bath. When one of them picked up both bracelets and slipped them over her wrist, Gladys felt a shiver of panic.

'Don't play games,' she said, 'or you'll go to bed without any telly.'

Her panic soared. The girl with the bracelets had taken both off and handed them to the other girl.

'Don't do that!' Gladys screamed as the other girl put a bracelet on each wrist. She leapt forward, seized her arms, and wrenched the bracelets off. She held them out, one in each hand. 'Now put them on properly!'

They stood like statues, naked and unmoving. She tried to

outstare them, but their cold, hostile eyes were too painful to bear and she lowered her head. 'Please,' she begged.

They stepped forward, took a bracelet each and put it on their wrist. Then, smiling at each other, and at Gladys, they began to dress.

She watched them sadly. There was no way of telling if they had taken their own bracelets, and she was overcome by a deep sense of loss. She knew, from the times she had examined them all over – looking for a mole or a blemish to distinguish one from the other – that she didn't know which was which. Now she never would. And for all she knew, they had been fooling her with their bracelets ever since they started addressing each other as 'Georgie'.

Tearfully, she told a friend, 'I should've had their names tattooed on their bums soon as they was christened.'

In the interview room at Colchester police station Millson asked Roger North where he'd spent the night with the Habenhowe twins.

'At their place,' North said. 'Pilcox Cottage. It's on the unmade road from Tanniford to Pilcox Hill.'

'Interview suspended at' – Millson glanced at his watch – 'nineteen-twenty-five. Excuse us for a moment,' he said to North, and with a jerk of his head at Scobie to follow him, stood up and left the room.

Outside in the corridor he asked, 'How quickly can you make Tanniford, Norris?'

'Ten . . . fifteen minutes.'

'Right. I want those Habenhowe girls questioned, and I want this alibi of his either broken or proved to the hilt. I'll keep him here until you phone in.'

Pilcox Cottage was a two-storey thatched cottage that stood alone at the top of Pilcox Hill. The rural setting was spoiled by a brick garage at the side of the cottage and the caravan next to it.

As Scobie drove on to the grass verge at the side of the road and parked, a tall figure emerged from the caravan and lumbered to the door of the cottage.

Beside Scobie, the WDC he'd hurriedly snatched from the canteen to accompany him reared up in her seat. 'I don't like the look of him, Sarge,' she said.

Scobie had been told about Hughie by Kathy. He was a backward boy the twins had befriended when they were little, and now worked for them as a kind of bodyguard. Hughie was twenty-six. In current jargon he had 'learning difficulties'. Before Georgina and Georgette moved to Pilcox Cottage he'd lived with his married sister, Carol. Kathy believed the reason the twins had taken him with them and bought a caravan for him was because Carol's husband, Lionel, refused to put up with him any longer.

'He's harmless unless you threaten the twins,' Scobie assured the policewoman, 'and then he's worse than a Rottweiler, I'm told.'

Before they reached the gate, the front door of the house opened to Hughie's knock and the twins stood in the door-way looking down the path. Scobie heard them say, 'It's all right, Hughie,' and Hughie turned and ambled back to the caravan.

The twins stood waiting. They wore black velvet skirts, black tank tops and black tights, and each had her name in gold letters on a brooch pinned to her left breast. Scobie realized he'd been expected when Georgina said, 'You've come to ask us about Roger,' as he and the policewoman showed their warrant cards.

'Yes,' he said. 'May we come in?'

'Of course.' They turned and led the way across a hall and into a lounge.

In contrast to the outside, the interior of the cottage was in modern style with concealed halogen lighting, and expensive furniture and fittings. Georgina and Georgette seated them-selves on the Knolle settee, their movements neat and pre-cise, sitting upright, knees together, hands in laps.

The WDC flopped untidily into an armchair. She was a plain girl in a grey anorak and navy-blue skirt, with lank, mouse-coloured hair. Her sloppiness made the twins' groomed hair and freshness all the more noticeable.

Scobie took another armchair, wondering how to begin.

Normal procedure required him to question them separately but, from all he'd heard about them from Kathy, he was almost certain they would refuse. He didn't see what he could do if they did, and decided to treat them as one witness.

'Would you mind telling us where you were around midnight last Wednesday night?' he asked.

'Here,' said Georgette. 'Roger arrived in a taxi just after half past one.'

'He stayed the night with us and left again in the morning to catch the eight o'clock train to London from Tanniford station,' said Georgina. 'That's what you want to know, isn't it?'

It seemed they had worked out exactly what to say and Scobie suspected Roger North was giving the same story to Millson. 'I'd like to know a little more than that,' he said. 'This is a murder investigation and it will take more than a couple of sentences to confirm Mr North's story.'

Their eyes rounded like saucers. 'Would you like us to tell you what he did with us?' Georgette asked pertly.

'No,' he said, irritated by the grin on the policewoman's face. 'I'd like to know if you were expecting him that night, or if he turned up by chance.'

'We invited him,' said Georgina.

'We phoned him in the afternoon,' said Georgette.

'I see. Do you often invite him to stay the night with you?'

He was laying himself open to a saucy answer, but he had to draw them out. The only way to upset the alibi was to uncover discrepancies between their version of events, and the one North was recounting to Millson.

'No. That was his first time,' said Georgina.

Scobie was thwarted. That put paid to his hope of catching North out with questions on a bogus relationship.

'He was very good,' said Georgette.

'Very good,' said Georgina.

Their blank expressions gave no hint of whether the innuendo was deliberate or not, but he suspected it was and they were taunting him.

Annoyed, he asked, 'Why didn't Mr North tell us this when we questioned him Saturday morning?'

'I expect he was protecting our reputation,' said Georgette. Their doll-like faces opened in simultaneous smiles, displaying perfect teeth.

Scobie's annoyance turned to anger. North's comment about them on Saturday hadn't indicated much concern in that direction. And their practice of speaking alternately – complementing each other's answers and mimicking the police procedure of two officers questioning a suspect – was winding him up. He'd even caught himself turning his head from one to the other like a suspect.

'Tell me about the taxi,' he demanded. 'Describe the vehicle and driver, please.'

'We didn't see it,' said Georgina.

'Only heard it drive away,' said Georgette.

Scobie clenched his teeth. As he racked his brains for what to ask next, they ostentatiously looked at their watches. 'We have to get changed now,' said Georgina.

'We have a date,' said Georgette. There was a whisper of velvet on nylon as they stood up.

Their utter confidence galled him, and he glanced helplessly at the WDC, hoping she might have a searching question to put, but she merely shrugged. Forcing a smile, he nodded and rose from the armchair.

As the front door closed behind him, he walked gloomily down the path to his car, the WDC trailing behind. He'd come away with nothing. He hadn't broken North's alibi, and neither had he proved it. His visit had been fruitless, not even turning up a minor deviation or discrepancy for George Millson to latch on to.

In the car, he reached for the handset with a frustrated sigh to report his failure to Millson.

'Cheer up, Sarge,' the WDC said sympathetically. 'They're just a couple of smart-arses. You'll get 'em another time.'

'I wouldn't put money on it,' Scobie muttered.

In the interview room, Millson, joined by a DC, had resumed his interrogation of Roger North. North said he'd known the twins all their lives, apart from a six-year gap after he'd left Tanniford to take a degree at Leeds. When he began using the house in Ferry Street again, Georgina and Georgette had called and hinted they'd be interested in having him spend a night with them.

'I was the only presentable male in the village they hadn't conquered,' he explained coyly to Millson. 'I escaped to university when I was nineteen, and didn't return.'

Last Wednesday, the twins phoned him at the office and issued a direct invitation. He was flattered, and explained he had a party that evening. They told him to come down after it, so he did. He'd taken the train to Colchester, as he said, and then a taxi to their cottage.

Scathingly, Millson told him the explanation was unbelievable. However, his efforts to shake the story failed. Roger stuck to it rigidly, repeating it parrot-fashion, careful to add nothing.

'Keep it simple, and don't add a thing,' Georgina had instructed. 'We'll do the same.'

'They can't *make* you say anything, Biggy,' said Georgette. 'They won't put you on the rack.'

Millson prodded at the only weakness. 'Why didn't you tell us this when we questioned you last Saturday, Mr North? Why say you came down to prepare for the weekend?'

'At the time, I didn't see any reason to involve Georgina and Georgette. I had no idea I would be suspected of murdering Trudy. Then when you started accusing me, I realized I had to tell the truth.'

'You know what I believe?' Millson said. 'I believe you never expected us to connect you with Trudy's pregnancy, and you've had to concoct this story on the hoof.'

'I haven't concocted it. It's the truth,' North said firmly.

He clung doggedly to his explanation as Millson took him through it again and when Millson was summoned from the room to receive Scobie's call, he was as irritated with Roger North as Scobie was with the twins. He listened to Scobie's negative report from mounting frustration.

'Is that all you could get out of them?' he demanded.

'Afraid so, sir.'

'Pah!' said Millson, and slammed down the phone.

Returning to the interview room he told North curtly, 'I'm

far from satisfied with the explanation of your movements Wednesday night, Mr North, and we shall be making further enquiries. For the moment, you're free to go.'

North nodded. He looked worried.

Scobie was depressed when he arrived home that evening. George Millson had been critical of his failure with the Habenhowe twins when he returned to the office, and had brushed aside his explanation of the difficulties.

Over the evening meal Kathy Benson asked, 'Why so glum, Norris?'

He sighed. 'George is pissed-off with me. He sent me to interview Georgina and Georgette Habenhowe and I didn't get the result he wanted. I've let him down.'

'Do you want to tell me about it?'

He didn't usually discuss his work with her, but he needed to air his frustration. 'They're such damned know-alls,' he said. 'And they made a fool of me. That double-act of theirs – speaking in turn – it really wound me up.'

'They do it deliberately,' Kathy said. 'It's to show you they're of one mind. And you'll find nothing one of them says ever conflicts with what the other has said. Why were you interviewing them?'

'Checking Roger North's alibi. He says he spent the night of the murder with them.'

'And you believed him?' Kathy's voice rose in derision. 'Norris, he doesn't even *like* them. If anything, he's afraid of them . . . always has been. The last thing he would do is to spend a night at their place.'

'But they confirmed his story. They said he did.'

She wrinkled her nose in disgust. 'That doesn't mean much. They lie in their teeth when it suits them.'

'Why would they lie about a thing like that?'

'I don't know, but they'll have a reason. You can be sure of that,' Kathy said.

CHAPTER 9

Millson's day began with a minor conflict at home. When he picked up his electric shaver in the bathroom that morning, the head was covered in hairs – full-size hairs, not beard stubble. Recalling the length of time his daughter had spent in the bathroom yesterday evening getting ready to go out, he stepped along to her bedroom.

'What have you been doing with my razor, young lady?'

'I borrowed it to shave my legs. I didn't think you'd mind. I blew all the hairs out.'

'You didn't, and I do. You shouldn't be shaving your legs at your age.' He wasn't sure whether she should or not.

'But they're hairy,' Dena wailed. 'Julie does. She's got a lady-shave razor.'

'Well, buy yourself a packet of throw-away razors out of your pocket money. They'll do the job just as well, and they're much cheaper.'

Over breakfast he voiced a thought he'd had earlier. 'I think it's time you had a weekend with your mother again, Dena.'

'Oh, no! Please, Dad. I can't stand that little horror, Terry. I promise I won't ever use your razor again.'

He restrained a laugh. He hadn't meant it as a threat, and he'd forgotten Dena detested his ex-wife's small son. 'Don't be daft, it's nothing to do with that. It's just that you're growing up and . . . well, maybe you need some advice . . .' She was regarding him with a puzzled frown. 'You know . . . girl problems,' he said uncomfortably.

Her face cleared. 'Oh, that. Don't worry, Dad, I phone Kathy if I have a problem. She's great. Anyway, I wouldn't ask Mum.'

It hadn't occurred to Millson that his daughter would consult Kathy Benson. He felt relieved. He was fond of Kathy, and trusted her. And at the office later, when Scobie mentioned his conversation with Kathy yesterday evening, he said, 'She's a good girl, your Kathy. What did she say, exactly?'

'That Roger North doesn't like the twins and certainly wouldn't spend the night with them. She thinks they're all lying.'

'Yes, well, so do I. But I can't for the life of me see why the Habenhowe girls would give North a false alibi.'

'To put him in their debt for some reason?' Scobie suggested.

'Yes, but what reason?' Millson rubbed his chin. 'Have someone dig into their background, Norris. See if there's a connection between them and Trudy Thornton.' He glanced at the clock on his wall. 'And ask the press liaison officer to arrange a press conference for eleven o'clock, and to have Trudy's mother there.'

Charles Howard finished *The Times* crossword that morning before his train reached Chelmsford, a record for him. He folded the paper and put it away in his briefcase. Laying his head back against the headrest, he indulged himself with memories of last night.

He'd been late arriving home and as a consequence he and Laura had had a late dinner. He'd kept his news until then. As he reached across the table with the wine bottle to fill his wife's glass, he said casually, 'Robert called me in this evening. That's why I was late.'

She looked up. 'What did he want?'

'I can expect an official note in a day or two. It won't take effect until Faulkner goes, of course, but I'll be taking over for him as Deputy Under Secretary of State.'

'Darling, that's wonderful! I'm so pleased!' Laura jumped up from her chair and came round the table to him. Putting her arms round his neck, she nuzzled his face with her cheek. 'I always knew I'd married a brilliant man.' She took his face in her hands and kissed him deeply, stirring him with her darting tongue.

78

He'd produced the Moet & Chandon from his briefcase.

'Champers! Oh, goody, I'll get the glasses!' Excitedly, she ran from the room.

He smiled. Success was an aphrodisiac to Laura. Should he tell her the best part now, or later? Later, he decided. In bed.

A bottle of champagne and several whiskies later, he took her to bed. She was giggly and provocative, reminding him of their first years of marriage. As he slipped into bed beside her he murmured, 'Shouldn't be surprised if there were a letter from the Lord Chamberlain's Office soon.'

'Oh, goody. Another garden party?'

'No, not a garden party,' he said teasingly.

She sat up quickly. 'What, then?'

'The Birthday Honours. A KCB.'

She squealed with delight. 'Charles! Oh, Charles!' She hurled herself on top of him, chanting: 'Sir Charles Howard and Lady Howard. Sir Charles Howard and Lady Howard.'

Later, in the aftermath of lovemaking, she murmured languidly, 'Lady Laura Howard.' She repeated it quietly to herself as he mounted her a second time.

Laura Howard had been exceptionally responsive to her husband that night.

Millson took Joyce Thornton into his office before the press conference began and told her they had found the place where her daughter had been killed. He explained where it was and asked if Trudy would have known the spot. He thought it possible the location hadn't been chosen at random and had significance – like being a previous courting place – which might be a clue to the killer's identity. Mrs Thornton seemed baffled by the question, and shook her head.

Millson regarded her compassionately. She seemed to have aged ten years since her daughter's murder a week ago. 'Would you be willing to make an appeal for information, Mrs Thornton?'

She nodded disconsolately. 'If it will help.'

'Oh, it'll help, all right,' he assured her. Now he had more

79

facts he wanted all the publicity he could get to unearth fresh witnesses, and there was nothing like a grieving mum for catching the eye of news editors.

Leaving her in the care of a policewoman, he went along to the conference room to address the media. Until now, he had refused interviews and channelled information to the media through a police spokeswoman, mainly because there had been so little of it. That hadn't hindered press speculation on the manner and place of Trudy's death: one tabloid had called it, 'THE A12 MURDER'.

He told the assembled reporters Trudy had been run down and killed in a lane near her home in Feering, and pointed it out on a large sketch map that had been placed on an easel beside him. He withheld the information that she had been deliberately run over a second time.

'Her body was then taken a short distance — almost certainly by car — to where the slip road from Feering joins the A12,' he went on. 'The driver probably parked in this lay-by' — he indicated it on the map — 'and then carried her body to the A12 carriageway and left it there to give the impression she had been killed in a hit-and-run accident.'

A reporter raised his arm. 'She *wasn't* killed on the A12, then?'

'That's what I've just said,' Millson said tartly, recognizing the reporter who had dubbed the case, 'THE A12 MURDER'. He went on, 'Trudy was seen leaving Kelvedon station and getting into a car at around midnight. We need to speak urgently to the driver of that car and I appeal to him to come forward so that he can be eliminated from our enquiries. We're also anxious to trace a taxi driver who may have picked up a man outside Colchester station at twenty past one in the morning and taken him to an address in the Tanniford area. It's possible his vehicle is not an authorized hire vehicle and I would stress that we're not concerned with that, we're only interested in any information he can give us about his passenger. And finally, Trudy was two months pregnant, and we need the man responsible to come forward. He may have no connection with her murder, but we need him to contact us so that we can eliminate him from our enquiries. Again, we will respect confidentiality.'

After dealing with questions, Millson had Trudy's mother brought in to make her appeal. She spoke haltingly, stumbling over her words. As she began to fold, tears flowing, he led her away, satisfied the item would make the national and regional television news.

In London that morning Roger North noticed a change in Charles Howard's demeanour, a more authoritative manner. Roger suspected the interview with the permanent secretary yesterday evening had been more than routine and that Charles had received confirmation of his impending promotion. The prospect made Roger even more nervous of him. Charles would crush him like a gnat if he found out he'd been hopping into bed with his wife every time he was away. In fact ... Roger shivered ... Charles Howard was quite likely to kill him.

He was startled when, in the middle of the morning briefing, Howard suddenly said, 'You look a bit peaky, Roger. Is anything the matter?' His cold blue eyes searched Roger's face.

'A little tired, sir, that's all.'

'Not worrying about anything?' Again the cold eyes raked his face.

'No, really.' He was worrying about everything at the moment. Not only Laura Howard, but yesterday evening with Georgina and Georgette Habenhowe.

They had picked him up outside Colchester police station in their ostentatious bronze sports car and taken him to the town's most exclusive Chinese restaurant. 'Our treat,' they said.

He was not dressed for an evening out and felt awkward as bow-tied Chinese waiters and waitresses in brilliantly coloured cheongsams hovered around them. From the smiles and the personal greeting by the manager, it was clear Georgina and Georgette were favoured customers.

They were wearing high-neck, ankle-length white dresses split to mid-thigh, and each of them wore an identity necklace bearing her name in gold letters. Their copper-coloured hair shone with lacquer and they were in full make-up.

Heads turned as they glided to their reserved table – slim goddesses in their white dresses and gold accoutrements. People were fascinated, as always, by their extraordinary likeness. The twins were used to being stared at – they'd been stared at all their lives – but Roger was uncomfortable under the public scrutiny that encompassed him as well. And he resented the envious glances of the men, although, ordinarily, he would have been pleased to be escorting two such striking girls. The twins weren't ordinary, however, and he wasn't escorting them – it was the other way round.

He left the ordering of the meal to them, accepting their suggestions, and allowing the activity and the discussion with the waiters to flow over him. He felt like a small boy who is not part of the proceedings. They had made him feel like that from a time when he *was* a small boy – the time in the churchyard at Tanniford. He cringed at the recollection. Every detail had been etched on his memory: the blue summer sky, the green grass of the churchyard, the dark green of the big holly bush in the corner, and the red brick wall behind it.

Out of sight in that corner behind the bush, eleven-year-old Roger and his friend, Timmy, had been discovering what all young boys discover about themselves sooner or later. At a critical moment the Habenhowe twins, who had been watching through the holly bush, burst in upon them. As they hurriedly covered up, tucking in shirts and zipping up trousers, the nine-year-old girls stood giggling and pointing.

'Take it out and show us again,' they demanded.

Timmy obliged readily, but Roger refused and turned to go. The twins whistled and Hughie appeared from the other side of the bush to prevent his escape. Big Hughie, a giant of a boy, who did everything they told him to, and whose large hands could twist your arm until you screamed.

'If you don't do as we say, we'll tell your mum,' said one twin.

'And we'll tell the Reverend Gaye what you've been doing in his churchyard,' said the other.

Roger imagined himself being damned in church. 'An abomination has been committed!' the vicar would thunder from the pulpit next Sunday. 'Hellfire and damnation will follow as surely as the sun shall rise in the morning.'

Roger thought his father would probably understand, but his mother certainly wouldn't. And you didn't tangle with Big Hughie, not if you had any sense. He was queer in the head.

Ashamed and humiliated – the humiliation angered him whenever he thought of it – he'd obeyed. The examination and handling by two curious girls had brought an inevitable response, and from then on it had been their nickname for him. In time it became like a hypnotic keyword, reinforcing the memory of his shame and subjugation. 'I can't think why those girls call you "Biggy",' his mother used to say. 'You're not big at all.'

He was rudely returned to the present by a finger prodding him in the chest. 'What'll you have to drink, Biggy?' Georgina asked.

'White wine, please . . . dry.'

'OK.' She ran a finger down the wine list then looked up. A wine waiter flew to her side and took the order.

The meal was served and Roger watched them attack the dishes with chopsticks, competently transferring food to their bowls, then holding the bowls to their mouths like the Chinese and dexterously flicking the food in. Furtively, he took up his own implements. '*He'll* have a spoon and fork,' they'd told the waiter when they ordered.

After the meal, sipping China tea, they told him what they wanted him to do in return for keeping his secret and providing an alibi for Wednesday night. It involved spending next weekend at Pilcox Cottage. 'And this time you really will spend the night with us. What we want you to do . . .'

His eyes widened in shock as they explained what was required of him. It was bizarre. He searched their faces to see if it was a joke. It wasn't. They were absolutely serious.

He was still in shock when they delivered him to Colchester station for the train back to London.

83

On the platform they had gaily waved him goodbye with a, 'See you on Saturday, Biggy.'

In the evening, Laura Howard phoned Roger at his flat. He had been dreading a call from her, wondering how he would put her off coming to Tanniford on Saturday again, now that he was committed to spending the weekend with Georgina and Georgette. He knew Charles would be away in Brussels, and as he picked up the phone and heard her voice, he tried desperately to think of an excuse.

He was saved by her opening words. 'We have to cool things for a while, poppet. I think Charles is becoming suspicious.'

Following the momentous news Charles had given her last night, Laura had decided to shelve her affair with Roger for the moment. He'd been a pleasant diversion, but now she must behave herself and take not the slightest risk of jeopardizing her future. In fact, contemplating Charles's forthcoming summons to the Palace, and her future elevated status, she wasn't sure she would resume the affair. After all, Roger was a mere principal, an underling in her husband's office.

'So take care of yourself, sweetie,' Laura ended. 'And I'll ring you sometime.'   .

Roger was relieved about the weekend, but piqued that Laura had dropped him so abruptly. No farewell dinner, no fond goodbye. Just a brief phone call. He didn't believe her explanation about Charles. That was simply an excuse to end the affair. He wondered if she'd found someone else. Probably, he thought.

At least now he needn't feel he was betraying her with Georgina and Georgette – although that was a small matter alongside his worry over what they might be involving him in. Was that their real reason for wanting him there this weekend? And why had they taken the trouble to gain a hold over him, so that he dare not refuse their invitation?

84

CHAPTER 10

In the routine procedures of the incident room every name associated with the investigation was logged and added to the computer data bank. The names were then run against the Criminal Record Index on the Police National Computer and against local records, and a report issued on any that found a match.

On Friday morning, following Scobie's interview of him the previous Tuesday, Frank Worseley's name found a match in local records. The file was located in the general office and brought to Scobie by the collator.

'There've been some complaints against that builder bloke you interviewed, Sarge.'

'Bad workmanship?'

The collator smirked. 'More like the wrong kind of work. Two complaints of indecent assault and one of alleged rape.'

'Let me see.' Scobie took the file from him and scanned the notes. 'Who was the investigating officer?'

'WDC King.'

'Ask her to come and see me.'

Scobie continued reading. The incidents had a common thread: Worseley working where the woman was alone . . . no witnesses . . . the women unwilling to appear in court . . . no further action. In the case of the alleged rape, the victim had agreed to give evidence at first and then changed her mind.

'Why did she change her mind?' Scobie asked the WDC when she reported to him.

'She was married but separated, Sarge, and she had a kiddie. She was afraid Worseley would say she consented, and she might lose custody of the child if her husband got wind of it.'

'You questioned Worseley?'

'Yes. He denied rape and said just what the victim was afraid he would. He said she agreed to sex.'

'What did you think of him?'

She made a face. 'Brains between his legs . . . thinks he's God's gift to women . . . and guilty as hell.' She shrugged. 'But he'd no previous and the DI said CPS wouldn't look at the case without her evidence, or without corroboration, so we had to leave it.'

Scobie grinned at her. 'I think we've just uncovered a new lead in the murder investigation, Constable.'

George Millson was suffering a mid-morning craving for a cigarette. He was concentrating his mind on the benefits of not smoking, and scowled at Scobie for interrupting him.

'Suppose – just suppose,' Scobie said eagerly, 'that it wasn't Roger North who made Trudy Thornton pregnant.'

'Who did then, the fairies?' Millson asked caustically.

'He's no fairy,' Scobie said. 'He's a muscular builder called Frank Worseley . . . the man who fitted Trudy's kitchen.'

'Any evidence for this?'

'Not direct, no, but there's a file on him. Complaints of indecent assaults and rape. Didn't get to court.' Scobie warmed to his theme. 'Seems he can't keep his hands off a woman who's on her own where he's working. He's not bad-looking . . . good physique, so maybe they don't all complain. Suppose he tried it on with Trudy, and she didn't resist? Or else didn't fight hard enough and – as with these other women – she didn't like to do anything about it. That would explain why she didn't tell anyone. Then, when she found she was pregnant, she told him she was going to the police, and he killed her.'

Millson gave Scobie a wry smile. 'That's a mighty long speech for you, Norris. And a mighty lot of speculation, too.'

He leaned back in his chair and clasped his hands together. This was when he missed a cigarette most – when he wanted to cogitate. Restlessly, he sat forward again. 'OK, follow it up. Speak to Trudy's neighbours. They might know if any funny business went on while Worseley was there over Easter. And have a word with the Child Support Agency. If

Worseley has been dipping his wick all over the place, they might be chasing him for maintenance. That would lend weight to your theory.'

Vera Munnings, the old lady living in the house next to Trudy's, remembered Frank Worseley well. 'Cocky young blighter. Liked showing off his body,' she told Scobie. She gave a titter. 'Tried to chat me up when I wen' in the garden.'

'What was he like with Trudy?'

'I reckon he fancied her. All the time she was on her sunbed sunning herself, he kep' eyeing her up.'

'D'you think he did anything about it?' Scobie asked.

'Fancy you wanting to know that.' Old Vera sniggered. 'Reckon he did, 'cos on the Monday . . .'

Worseley had been in the garden, shaping the worktop, taking it in, and bringing it out again, planing and sawing it, to make it fit. It was the most difficult part of the job, he told Vera. Trudy had called him into the house for a cup of tea and, a while later, Vera went indoors to make one herself.

'I heard noises next door,' she said. 'Sounded like Trudy was hollering. So I puts me ear to the wall . . .' Vera went to the wall and demonstrated. 'These cottages used to be one, see, and this is only plasterboard.' Her face came away from the wall with a knowing expression. 'They w's bonking,' she cackled. 'I haven't forgot what bonking sounds like.'

'Are you sure he wasn't raping her?' Scobie asked.

Vera gave him a look. 'Can't say as to that, can I? She looked a bit flustered when she come out again later.'

'Upset?'

The old lady wasn't committing herself. 'Hot and bothered – like she'd just been tumbled. That's what we called it in my young day.'

Scobie reported to Millson the following morning. 'The way Vera Munnings told it, Trudy may have been willing,' he said. 'And I've spoken to the CSA. Two women have named Frank Worseley as the father of their kids. He denies they're his, and the CSA have asked for a DNA test. Looks hopeful, doesn't it?'

Millson nodded. 'Willing or not, what matters is whether he made her pregnant,' Millson said. 'If he did, the fact he hasn't come forward makes him a suspect for her murder. I want him in for questioning.'

To Scobie's surprise, the message on Worseley's answerphone said he was working at The Lawns in West Bergholt, Charles Howard's address. He drove out there, accompanied by a DC.

Worseley was up a ladder attending to the guttering at the side of the house when they turned into the drive. Scobie parked alongside Worseley's black Ford Transit and as he got out of the car to summon him down, Laura Howard came out of the French windows on to the patio. It was a sweltering June day and she was wearing a sun-dress. It hung loosely from the shoulders, but stretched tightly over her generous breasts, outlining the nipples and making it apparent she was not wearing a bra.

She frowned at Scobie, but her manner was not so domineering as last week. 'Can I help you, Sergeant?'

Again he was intrigued by her voice. He felt he could listen to those mellifluous tones without bothering about the words, and simply enjoying their clarity and musicality.

'You have a Mr Worseley working here, Mrs Howard,' he said. 'I'd like a word with him, please.'

She arched her eyebrows. 'He's up there.' She pointed at the ladder and swished back inside.

The DC whistled to attract Worseley's attention and signalled him to come down. He descended the ladder slowly, his body above the tattered shorts glistening with sweat.

'What d'you want this time?' He glared at Scobie.

'We'd like you to come down to the station and answer some questions.'

'What about?'

'We think you can help us with our enquiries into the murder of Trudy Thornton.'

'Murder? I don't know nothing about no murder.'

'It would be better if you came of your own accord,' Scobie

88

said firmly, as the DC stepped forward ready to arrest and caution him if he refused.

'OK,' Worseley said sulkily, 'I get the message. I'll have to let Mrs Howard know, though. She won't like you taking me off the job.' He stepped in through the French windows. A moment later he came out again, preceded by Laura Howard.

'How long is he going to be?' she asked Scobie.

'I'm afraid I can't say.'

She clicked her tongue. 'This is very irritating.' She turned to Worseley. 'Make sure you dock the time from your bill, then.'

'Yes, madam.' Behind her back as she returned inside, he gave an exaggerated display of touching his forelock.

'How do you come to be working here?' Scobie asked as they walked to the car.

'She got me from Yellow Pages. I don't only fit kitchens, you know.'

In the interview room, Scobie started the tape recorder and dictated the date and time and who was present.

Millson began in a friendly tone. 'Mr Worseley, I understand you do odd jobs all over the place . . . fitting kitchens . . . repairing gutters and so on?'

'Yeah, I can turn me hand to most things.'

Millson nodded and smiled encouragingly. 'And I suppose sometimes you find yourself with a woman alone in the house . . . she's a bit bored perhaps . . . and a good-looking lad like you gets propositioned, eh?'

'Yeah, it happens.' Worseley had relaxed enough to grin. 'And some of 'em are after a bit of discount off the bill.'

'And I'll bet you give it to them, don't you?'

'Yeah, why not? If they's willing.'

'And they need a little persuasion sometimes?'

'I ain't never forced a tart. Look, I know what you're on about. I had all this last year with them other birds and it was cleared up.'

'Not *cleared up*,' Millson said firmly. 'Not proceeded with. There's a big difference.'

'Yeah, all right. But like I said then . . . some birds say no when they mean yes. Then they feel guilty after, so they say they was forced.'

'What about Trudy Thornton?' Millson snapped. 'Did she say no when she meant yes?'

Worseley's eyes flared with alarm. 'I never had it off with her!' he said quickly.

'Put up a fight, did she?'

'I never did nothing with her, I tell you.' Worseley, who was still only wearing shorts, was visibly sweating.

Millson remained silent, letting him stew. After a while Worseley said, 'Look, can I have a fag?'

Millson hadn't had a cigarette for two weeks and wasn't sure he could survive watching Worseley light up and smoke. He was tempted to say, 'Not yet.' However, the man was not in custody and he was not under arrest. So either he had to let him smoke, or suspend the interview and lose the momentum. Reluctantly, he said, 'Yes, if you must.'

As Worseley went through the ritual of lighting up, Millson went on, 'You've been pretty careless with some of your conquests, haven't you? The CSA are chasing you for child maintenance, I gather.'

Worseley inhaled and blew out smoke. 'It's not me that's careless, guv'nor. I leave protection to the birds. They're wised up, these days. That's why I'm contesting, see? Those kids ain't mine.'

Millson nodded amiably. The crisis was over and the craving for a cigarette had passed. 'Trudy Thornton was pregnant too, you see.'

'Yeah, I read it. That ain't nothing to do with me.'

'Isn't it? According to a specialist in these matters she conceived over Easter. And – on your own evidence – you were the only man who was around then.'

Worseley's face, which had relaxed again, suddenly stiffened. 'What about the nights? I wasn't there then.'

'Nor was anyone else so far as we know. Anyway,' Millson said casually, 'we can easily resolve this with a DNA test. You understand what that is?'

'Yeah, the CSA were on about one. You need a sample for that and I ain't giving one. You can't make me.'

Millson felt a quiet elation. Worseley's refusal – before he'd even been asked – confirmed his suspicion.

'You're not right about that, old son,' he said. 'We can't take *intimate* samples – like semen or blood – without your consent, but we *can* take non-intimate samples without consent. Hair, for instance, though not pubic hair.' Seeing Worseley's eyes widen in anxiety, he pressed the point home. 'So, all we need is a hair from your head. The scientists will make a genetic analysis . . . compare it with the foetus . . . and *prove* that you fathered it.'

Millson sat back with folded arms, satisfied he'd driven Worseley into a corner.

Frank Worseley lowered his eyes and stared down at the table. He drew hard on his cigarette, the smoke wafting across and invading Millson's nostrils. Millson steeled himself, determined not to break the tension. After a moment Worseley's shoulders sagged and he muttered, 'Yeah, OK. It was me put her in the pudding club.'

Millson relaxed. A breakthrough. 'Caution him, Sergeant,' he said crisply.

Scobie leaned forward. 'Frank Worseley, you do not have to say anything. But it may harm your defence if you do not mention, when questioned, something which you later rely on in court. Anything you do say may be given in evidence.'

Worseley looked puzzled. 'You arresting me, then?'

'No, you're not under arrest,' Millson said, 'but you *are* under suspicion and you've been cautioned because I intend to ask you further questions. Are you willing to answer them?'

'Yeah, OK.' Worseley's voice was subdued.

'Let's start with Easter Monday. What happened between you and Trudy?'

He shrugged. 'She was giving me the old come-on, so . . . after a bit . . . I give it to her.'

'You mean you raped her,' Millson said.

'No, I didn't! She wanted to really . . . and once we started she was away. Wasn't my fault she hadn't got her diaphragm in.'

Millson restrained himself with difficulty. The best he

could do for Trudy now was to wring the truth from this slob, and nail him for her murder.

'She told you that?'

'Yeah, when she phoned me 'bout a month after an' told me she had a bun in the oven. She said she'd had a test, and we'd got to meet and talk.'

'Go on.'

'We met in a pub for a drink. She wanted me to accept the kid as mine – put my name on the birth certificate, like – and pay for its keep.'

'What did you say to that?'

Worseley shifted in his seat. 'I told her it was her own fault she was in the club an' to get rid of it.'

'How did she take it?'

'Called me a murderer an' said she was going to have it.' Worseley looked up and met Millson's eye. 'If you want my opinion, she *wanted* a baby. An' she wanted some mug to pay for it.'

'I *don't* want your opinion,' Millson growled. 'What happened then?'

'Nothing. I ran her back home.'

'I don't believe you!' Millson snarled. He leaned forward, his face close to Worseley's. 'I'll tell you what I think. Trudy wasn't some timid housewife like your other victims. She was going to report the rape . . . see it through to court . . . and have you put away. You couldn't risk that, so you met her at Kelvedon station last Wednesday week and tried to talk her out of it. She wouldn't listen. There was a row . . . she jumped out . . . and you drove after her and ran her down.'

'No! I wouldn't do a thing like that! I never see'd her again!' Worseley was shaking.

'Then why didn't you answer our appeals? You knew we were looking for the man who made her pregnant.'

''Cos I didn't have nothing to do with her murder,' Worseley said earnestly, 'an' I was in enough trouble with the other birds.'

'What sort of car do you drive?'

'Ain't got a car – I use a van.'

'It's a black Ford Transit,' Scobie told Millson. 'It could be mistaken for a large car in the dark.'

Millson nodded. 'Where were you between midnight and one o'clock last Wednesday week?'

'Home in bed.'

'Anyone to verify that?'

'No, I'm on me own.' Worseley saw Millson give Scobie a meaningful look and went on desperately, 'Listen, guv, I *didn't* meet Trudy and I *didn't* kill her. You gotta believe me!'

'You expect me to believe that after you refused to help her, she just left it at that? You'd raped her . . . made her pregnant . . . and she was going to have the baby and say nothing? Never. She was a respectable woman in a good job. How was she going to explain a baby?'

Worseley said eagerly, 'She said she'd have to unload it on someone else . . . tell some other guy it was his.'

'Who?'

'I dunno. Some guy she was going with, I think.'

'Did she mention a name?'

'No . . .' Worseley paused, then shook his head. 'No, she didn't.'

Millson remained silent, considering whether Worseley was acting and had the imagination to invent an answer like that. He concluded it was unlikely and that he was probably telling the truth. The man was just an ignorant lout who took advantage of defenceless women.

Reluctantly, he said, 'All right, you can go. But until we establish the truth of what you've told us, you remain a suspect. And you don't go on any long journeys without telling us. Understand?'

Worseley nodded and stood up looking shaken. He hesitated, as though about to speak, and then walked out of the room.

'You've let him go,' Scobie said accusingly. 'I thought he was a better suspect than Roger North.'

'And I think he was telling the truth about Trudy intending to blame the pregnancy on someone else. Tell me, Norris, who would she choose who would be most likely to believe her?'

'Roger North, I suppose,' Scobie said grudgingly.

'Precisely,' said Millson. 'And he had a motive. His career blighted and he'd be lumbered with Trudy and a baby. Whereas Worseley was facing nothing worse than he'd faced and got away with before – alleged rape and alleged fatherhood. I don't think he'd have killed her for that.'

CHAPTER 11

Roger North caught an early train to Tanniford on Saturday morning. It was going to be another gloriously sunny day and for a while as the train traversed the Essex countryside, he put aside his doubts and convinced himself it would be a fun weekend. That Georgina and Georgette were not the witches he thought they were, and he was exaggerating his fears.

But then, as the train neared Tanniford, he remembered their sixteenth birthday.

That was the summer he'd left school and was waiting to go up to university. He was surprised to receive the invitation to Georgina and Georgette's birthday party because he hadn't had anything to do with them for some time. He'd heard plenty about them, though. They were the talk of Tanniford.

The party was held in an upstairs room of the Black Dog and Gladys Habenhowe was there, looking grey and wrinkled beside her attractive young daughters. They were wearing lilac-coloured trouser suits, he remembered, with bow-ties to match, and white frill-fronted shirts.

'Sweet sixteen and never been kissed,' burbled middle-aged Lionel French as he arrived and they stepped forward to greet him. 'Soon put that right.'

Roger watched with amusement as he gripped their shoulders in turn and thrust his face forward, trying to kiss their lips. Each twin inclined her head at the last moment and diverted the kiss to her cheek.

Disappointed, Lionel said sarcastically, 'I s'pose you're wearing them name brooches so I know which of you I haven't kissed.'

A voice whispered in Roger's ear, 'What he don't know is they'll swap 'em over next time they go to the loo.'

Roger turned to find Gladys Habenhowe beside him. 'Why will they do that?' he asked.

'Same reason they call each other Georgie. So no one can tell t'other from which.'

'But surely *you* can, Mrs Habenhowe?'

'Oh no, lad.' Gladys sighed heavily, breathing fumes of alcohol in his face. 'Not since I used to tie labels on 'em when they was babies.'

Roger was surprised. Everyone in Tanniford knew Gladys had problems with her daughters, and that was why she'd taken to drink, but it hadn't occurred to him this was one of the problems. Roger believed he had a way of his own for distinguishing between Georgina and Georgette.

The winter before last, when he belonged to the local youth club, he'd often encountered the twins there. He found he could distinguish Georgette from Georgina by the slightly different way she looked at him. The difference was barely perceptible, but Georgette's eyes were softer and less distant than her sister's when they met his.

So far as he could discover, this response only occurred with him and not with other boys she talked to. He contemplated asking Georgette for a date to find out if she fancied him, but was put off by Dr Oakleigh who overheard him discussing her with his son, Robert.

'The Habenhowe girls are clones – near freaks – thanks to the foolish way their mother brought them up,' he told Roger. 'Don't try to come between them by asking Georgette without Georgina. Anyway, she won't accept.'

Roger had looked for that difference in Georgette when he arrived this evening, and they greeted him wearing name brooches. The one with the *Georgina* brooch said, 'You're still on our hit list, you know, Biggy.'

He knew what she meant – his name was on a list of boys who hadn't yet taken them out. The expression in her eyes was neutral. He glanced at the other girl and saw the warmth in her eyes as she returned his gaze. It was Georgette. They were displaying their own names.

Later, he used another test. Georgette had always been more relaxed, standing a shade closer to him than her sister, when they spoke. Several times during the evening he made a point of speaking to them and was confident he'd correctly identified Georgette each time. He even knew they'd exchanged brooches twice.

As the party broke up and he was about to leave they intercepted him. 'We'd like you to walk us home, please,' said Georgina.

Roger guessed what they were up to and thought it would be a laugh to string them along, and then confound them with his expertise.

'What about your mother?' he asked. Gladys Habenhowe, glass in hand, was slumped in a chair on the other side of the room.

'She'll be here till the bar closes,' Georgina said.

'Big Hughie will see her home,' said Georgette.

Gladys's bleary eyes watched them leave. She'd thought Roger would take young Auriol French home, and wondered why he'd allowed himself to be snared by Georgina and Georgette. Perhaps the boy had been put off by Auriol's father.

Gladys took a swig of her whisky. Miserable bugger, Lionel French. Poor Carol, having to put up with him for a husband. But beggars can't be choosers, as her mother used to say. And Carol had been desperate, begging Gladys for help when her parents turned her out. Seventeen . . . pregnant . . . and wouldn't say who the father was. Never had.

Gladys had been pregnant herself at the time, and felt sorry for the girl. She'd fixed her up with a place to have the baby far away from Tanniford. That was where the silly girl had met Lionel French and given herself to him in return for marriage and a name for the baby. He'd had the best of that bargain, all right, Gladys reckoned. Still, give the devil his due, he had allowed Carol's young brother, Hughie, to come and live with them when her parents wouldn't keep him any longer. Carol had probably had to make up to him for that, though.

97

Gladys heaved a mammoth sigh. Sad, sad world. She took another gulp of whisky.

At their house in West Street, where the door opened directly into the front room, Georgette stepped forward and sat down on the sofa. Georgina hung back, and as Roger waited politely, she locked the door and stood with her back against it.

'Got you at last, Biggy,' she said.

'Don't call me that! I don't like it,' he said, as a subliminal glimpse of the holly bush in Tanniford churchyard flashed before him.

'Come and sit down, Biggy,' said Georgette, ignoring his request, and patting the space beside her on the sofa.

That was when he noticed they were no longer wearing their name brooches. So much the better, he thought. They'll flip when I call them by their right names.

He sat down next to her and Georgina came and sat on the other side of him. 'A little bird has told us you're leaving Tanniford next month,' she said.

'Yes, I'm going up to Leeds University,' he said proudly.

'Do you know why you're on our list?' she asked.

'Because I'm the only boy in Tanniford who doesn't come running when you whistle,' he said.

'So, what's the matter with you?' Georgette asked. 'Are you gay?'

'Of course not,' he said sharply.

'That's good.' They leaned forward and grinned across him at each other. 'Bo-bo, Georgie?' said one. 'Zizzyplonk, Georgie,' said the other.

Roger had no idea what 'zizzyplonk' meant, but he knew 'bo-bo' was twinspeak for bed. It was time to drop his bombshell and leave. Time to pay them out for humiliating him.

'You can cut the Georgie stuff,' he said. 'I know perfectly well which of you is which. I've known for some time.'

There was a sudden stillness in the room. And then he felt the cold. It was a warm summer evening yet he was sure the temperature of the room had fallen. He looked at them. Their pale-blue eyes were alight with malice.

He jumped up from the sofa in alarm, only now recalling the rest of Dr Oakleigh's strange warning: *Don't ever threaten their oneness. They might react violently.*

They rose from the sofa as one and advanced on him. He backed away towards the locked door, aware this was no game. He was eighteen, a full-back at rugby, and it was ridiculous to be afraid of two sixteen-year-old girls, he told himself. But the malevolence of their faces frightened him.

He continued retreating until he was backed up against the door and they stood, heads together, with their faces inches from his own.

'Go on then,' one of them challenged. 'Who am I? Georgina or Georgette?'

Fearfully, he looked at the two pairs of eyes. They were equally venomous. 'I don't know!' he cried, and wouldn't have dared tell them if he did. 'It was a joke,' he said frantically. 'I didn't mean to upset you. I've got to go.'

He'd reached up behind him to the key and managed to unlock the door. Turning quickly, he yanked it open, and fled.

He hadn't come face to face with them again until they came to his house the Saturday the police called.

Frank Worseley had not had time to finish the job at The Lawns after his interview at Colchester police station the previous afternoon. He returned there on Saturday morning to complete the work.

'There'll be no extra charge for working Saturday, missus,' he told Laura Howard as he sat in the kitchen sipping the mug of tea she'd given him mid-morning.

'I should hope not,' she said, setting a coffee pot and cup and saucer on a tray for herself. 'What did the police want you for yesterday? Was it about the A12 murder?'

'Yeah.' He took a mouthful of tea and regarded her curiously. 'You knew that copper who came, didn't you, missus?'

She shrugged. 'He was here last week with another officer. The murdered woman was my husband's secretary and they wanted to find out what sort of person she was.'

'Cor, fancy that.' Frank Worseley's eyebrows lifted.

'So why did they want to see you?' Laura asked.

'It was 'cos I was working at her place a coupla months back an' they thought I was the guy who put her up the spout.'

'I beg your pardon?'

'Put a bun in her oven . . . made her preggers.'

Laura Howard's eyebrows arched disdainfully. 'I see. Why should they think that?'

Frank Worseley saw no reason to give himself a bad name by letting on he was the one who had lumbered Trudy with a baby. 'Well, they reckon she was put in pod around Eastertime, an' that was when I was there. It *weren't* me, of course, an' I soon put 'em right on that!'

Laura lifted the coffee pot and poured herself a cup. 'Was that all?' she asked casually. 'You were there for hours.'

'Yeah, well . . . they asked me other things too. Like, did I know who *had* put it up her.'

Laura brought her cup and sat down next to him at the table. 'How would *you* know that?'

He sensed a change in her manner, a slight alarm, and wondered what had caused it. ''Cos Trudy an' me met up about a month after, an' she told me she were preggers,' he said. 'The coppers thought she might have given a hint who the guy was.'

'And did she?' She took a sip of coffee, her blue eyes smiling encouragingly at him over the top of her cup.

'Not by name,' he said, watching her face. She was hanging on his words, lips parted, and holding her breath. Suddenly, he understood the reason for her anxiety . . . or thought he did.

He put down his mug, pleased with his intuition. This snooty tart was worried hubby had done it . . . knocked up his secretary. That's what it was. Maybe she knew he'd been having it off with her, and was afraid it would get to the papers. That's why she was probing what he knew, flashing those big blue eyes at him. Well, well. He'd string her along and see where it led.

He went on, 'Thinking about it, though, I might be able

100

to work out who Trudy meant.' He saw her eyes pop, and was sure now that he was right.

Trudy *had* said something to him that could identify who she was going to lumber with the baby. He'd remembered it soon after the police interview, but Millson had left when he phoned in, so he'd said he'd ring again. He didn't have to, though.

He looked her over. She was a big piece . . . good-looking . . . classy . . . and hubby was away this weekend. Frank Worseley licked his lips. Maybe . . . if he played his cards right . . .

Roger North was pleasantly surprised to find Georgina and Georgette waiting for him in the Saab as he came out through the ticket office at Tanniford station. He'd expected to have to trudge up the hill to Pilcox Cottage on foot.

They greeted him politely, with none of their usual mockery, as though he were a genuine invited guest arriving for the weekend.

On arrival at Pilcox Cottage he looked around curiously as he stepped into the hallway. He'd never seen inside before. A good thing the police hadn't known that when they questioned him, he thought. If they had, and had challenged him to describe the bedroom, for instance, they'd have discovered he couldn't have spent the night of the murder with the Habenhowe twins.

He took in the sumptuous interior, the hi-fi equipment and the superior kitchen, and reflected on one of the mysteries about the twins that intrigued everyone in Tanniford. It had arisen when they bought Pilcox Cottage and moved from the weatherboard house in West Street after their mother died. The village wondered how the twins had suddenly become rich and why they had taken Hughie Cole with them and bought him a caravan.

One rumour was that they had blackmailed a wealthy City financier. Another that Gladys Habenhowe had hoarded all the insurance money she received on Harry Habenhowe's death. There was doubt about that, though, because it seemed likely Gladys had spent it all on drink. It was commonly believed Gladys had drunk herself to death, driven to it by her crazy twin daughters.

Georgina and Georgette's wealth was no mystery to Roger. His father was a partner in the firm of solicitors that had acted for the twins on their mother's death. There had been an unusual double indemnity clause in the insurance policy the trawler company took out on Harry Habenhowe's life. On his death, his widow received two hundred thousand pounds. But if she too died before his children reached the age of eighteen, the children received a further two hundred thousand pounds each. Gladys Habenhowe had died five months before their eighteenth birthday.

The insurance company had contested the claim, citing the clause about 'a known medical condition', and alleging Gladys died of cirrhosis of the liver caused by alcohol abuse. The twins retaliated by hiring a smart lawyer who took the insurance company to court on their behalf and won. In addition to that money, Georgina and Georgette inherited the two hundred thousand their mother had received on their father's death. Gladys hadn't spent a penny of it. She'd invested the money and lived on the income.

Roger North peered around like a voyeur as he followed the twins upstairs and they showed him the guest bedroom with its king-size bed. There had been many tales about them, and about Hughie, and now here he was in their home, satisfying his own prurient curiosity.

On his way along the landing to the stairs after he'd unpacked, he peeped into their bedroom. It was meticulously tidy, the twin beds covered with matching duvets. Nothing sinister or erotic there. He descended the stairs, reassured to find them oddly courteous and polite, treating him like a guest and asking him if he had everything he wanted.

While he'd been unpacking they had changed into white slacks and navy blazers, their name brooches pinned to the lapels. 'We're taking you for a trip up to Pinmill on *Gigi* for lunch at the Butt and Oyster,' said Georgina.

He nodded appreciatively. *Gigi* was their luxurious motor-cruiser. She was berthed at the marina on the Walton Back-waters, a sleek vessel powered by twin 300-horsepower

Volvo Penta engines that gave her a speed of forty knots. Her technical details were well known in the yacht club, but few people had enjoyed the privilege of a trip on her and Roger looked forward to the experience.

Stepping on board at the marina he was relaxed, enjoying the invigorating air after the fume-laden streets of London. *Gigi*'s flying bridge was rather like a large open-top sports car. It was upholstered all round in leather, and there were two pedestal seats at the front with a wide bench-seat behind them. There was a roof canopy at the front and a control console either side of the wheel that had almost as many switches and gauges as an aeroplane.

Roger helped the girls to lower the roof canopy and then sat on the bench-seat and watched. Georgette cast off and, with Georgina at the helm, they piloted the big cruiser from her berth and through the moorings into the Twizzle. Then, with the two girls perched on the pedestal seats at the controls, *Gigi* purred sedately along Walton Channel and out past Stone Point.

Beyond Island Point buoy, Georgina stepped down from the helmsman's seat and said over her shoulder to Roger, 'Like to take her for a bit?'

He nodded eagerly and, climbing on to the seat next to Georgette, he grasped the wheel. Georgette opened the throttles and he felt the cruiser respond, the hull rising and planing the water as they sped towards the Pye End buoy.

'She's all yours now,' said Georgette, and stepped down from her seat to join her sister on the bench-seat behind him.

When Pye End buoy came abeam he gently turned the wheel to steer for the entrance to Harwich harbour. Suddenly, he became aware that Georgina was standing behind his seat.

'We'll run out to Gunfleet before we go into Harwich,' she said, and slipping her arms through his, she placed her hands over his on the wheel and turned it. As *Gigi* swung seaward, Georgette appeared beside him.

'Let's do a burn,' she said. Reaching out, she pushed both throttles wide open.

The cruiser responded like a scalded cat, leaping forward, the bow lifting like a plane taking off. Georgina had clamped his hands to the wheel with hers, and he dared not struggle. A jerk of the wheel at this speed would be disastrous. With the wind tearing his hair, Roger stared at the deserted sea ahead, mesmerized by the sensation of flying over the water.

In a quick movement, Georgette bobbed down and came up between him and the wheel, facing him. She put her arms round him and, from behind, Georgina put her mouth to his ear and shouted above the wind, 'Ever done it on the sea at forty knots, Biggy?'

Aghast, he shook his head.

'We have.' They both laughed.

They were insane, crazy like everyone said they were. Planing the water like this, a sudden movement of the wheel would flip the vessel over and they'd all be killed. Roger was terrified.

Georgette's face moved forward, eyes dancing, lips parted for an open-mouth kiss . . . and then they curved in a smile, and she burst out laughing.

'Your face!' Over his shoulder she said to her sister, 'His face, Georgie! He really believed it!' They both shrieked with merriment.

Georgette turned within his arms and, reaching out, slowly eased the throttles back. The cruiser came off the plane, down to displacement speed, then half speed, until finally she was stationary in the water, drifting with the tide.

Georgina released him from the wheel and Roger sagged in the seat. He was drenched with sweat inside his clothes, and furious at being made a fool of. They hadn't changed. It had been stupid of him to think they had. He felt a resurgence of worry about tonight.

'Don't look so upset, Roger,' said Georgina. 'It was only a joke.'

'Come below and have a drink,' said Georgette.

He nodded and smiled at them, but inside he was seething.

They put the cruiser on automatic pilot, setting a course slow ahead to the Cork, and after scanning the horizon, ushered him down the companionway to the sun-deck.

A while later, as he sipped a cocktail and gazed across the smooth sea, lulled by zephyrs of warm air on his cheek, Georgina said, 'We'll make it up to you tonight.'

'That's a promise,' said Georgette.

He smiled weakly, trying to persuade himself they were high-spirited, and this would be just another of their pranks. But the fear there was a sinister motive behind it remained.

At half past eleven on Saturday night George Millson started to worry. Dena was at a disco and had promised to be in by eleven. She always phoned to let him know if she was going to be late, and she hadn't done so this evening. He shut his mind to the cases of missing children he'd dealt with professionally, but when she walked in at midnight his relief exploded in anger.

'Where the hell have you been? Why didn't you phone?'

'Dad, I tried to, but I couldn't find a phone that worked.'

'I've been worried stiff,' he said.

'Dad, I was all right. I was having a nice time, and I didn't think you'd mind. You should have gone to bed.'

'How could I go to bed if you were still out?'

'Why not? I've got a key.' She sounded genuinely puzzled.

Millson was reminded of himself at her age, and a similar scene with his mother. Her frustrated: 'You just wait until *you're* a parent, George. Then you'll understand.'

His mother had been right, of course, although there was no point in saying the same thing to his daughter. Instead, he smiled wryly and said, 'You wouldn't understand, Dena. But don't ever do that to me again, or I'll take your key away.'

Later that night, in his bedroom above a converted garage at the bottom of Pilcox Hill, Frank Worseley was in bed. He lay on his back, a nylon sheet draped over the lower half of his naked body. He was in a deep, drunken sleep.

In the garage below were stored bags of cement, drainpipes and the accoutrements to his business. A door at the side opened into a hallway from where stairs led up to a landing and to his bedroom. At the foot of the stairs, as Worseley snored above, a flame flickered briefly. An instant later the flame rose and flashed up the stairs, following a trail of petrol to the foot of his bed and to the ring of petrol around it.

For a few moments Worseley slept on, oblivious of the danger. And then the heat ignited the nylon sheet. The burning material curled and melted in the way of man-made fibre, disintegrating around Worseley's body and sticking to the bare flesh. The searing pain jerked him from his drunken stupor.

Confused, he struggled up to find the bed encircled with flames and the room thick with smoke. He lurched to the window, fighting for breath. The window frame had been painted many times and was stuck fast to the sill. He reached for a chair and smashed the glass. Air surged in, bringing oxygen to the smouldering room. It exploded in a fireball.

Frank Worseley, his hair alight, stumbled around in the inferno. The searing heat stripped the skin from his eyelids and, blinded, he sank to the floor, screaming in agony. Within seconds his skin bubbled in the intense heat and his flesh began to char.

CHAPTER 12

Scobie's phone call to Millson, informing him Frank Worseley was dead, and it looked to be a case of murder, came at half past three in the morning. Millson dragged on his clothes and scrawled a note to Dena, leaving it on the kitchen table as he went out to his car.

The streets were deserted as he drove through Colchester to the Hythe and took the short route to Tanniford through the grounds of Essex University. He'd had less than three hours' sleep. He yawned and wondered if he'd been over-hasty with Dena last night. His job made it hard to be as relaxed as other fathers were about their daughters. He could see he'd soon have other problems he wasn't sure how to deal with, too . . . like boyfriends and wearing make-up. It was no use asking her mother. His ex-wife couldn't forgive him for Dena choosing to live with him instead of her.

'That's what you both wanted,' said Jean, the one and only time he'd sought her advice about their daughter. 'Now she's all yours . . . boys . . . the Pill . . . everything. Don't expect any help from me.'

Circling the first of the mini-roundabouts beyond the Hythe, he had the odd thought that his strongest memory of his ex-wife was her cold feet in bed.

An acrid smell of wet ash hung over the scene of the fire on the outskirts of Tanniford. He picked his way through the tangle of hoses and the yellow-helmeted firemen to a fire officer in a white helmet.

'How did it happen?' he asked, showing his identification.

'Someone torched him . . . the bedroom smells of petrol. The forensic boys are in there now making an examination. It looks as though he smashed the window to get out. Fatal, that is – people don't realize – and up it went. We were here within minutes of the call, but it was hopeless. He was burnt to a cinder when we got him out.'

'Who raised the alarm?'

'Your sergeant's with him now.' The fire officer pointed.

'Thanks.' Millson nodded and crossed the road to where Scobie stood speaking to a middle-aged man with grey hair.

'Morning, sir,' Scobie said as Millson approached. 'This gentleman was putting his car away after he got home about two o'clock this morning. He heard the smash of glass as Worseley broke the upstairs window.'

'The room went up like a bomb,' said the man. 'That's what I thought it was at first. Then I saw flames shooting out and ran into my house to phone.'

'Was there anyone else about?' Millson asked.

'No . . .' The man hesitated. 'Well, not right then. But as I came out again . . . to see if there was anything I could do . . . someone on a bike rode away from just opposite.'

Millson looked. 'There isn't anything there . . . only a hedge.'

'Yes, well, that's the thing, you see. I think they must have been there, in the shadow, all the time.'

'Watching, you mean?' Scobie asked.

'Well, they must have seen the fire, yet didn't do anything.'

Scobie took out his notebook. 'Can you describe this person?'

The man puckered his mouth in doubt. 'It was just a dark figure on a bike who rode away.'

'Man or woman?'

'Couldn't say. They were wearing a crash helmet, you see.'

'What sort of bike was it?' Scobie asked.

'I didn't really notice. Sports bike, I think. Went like the wind, it did.'

'Which way did it go?'

'That way.' The man pointed. 'Up Pilcox Hill.'

Before Scobie could ask the man another question, Millson said, 'Thank you,' and took Scobie's arm. 'Where's your car, Norris?'

'I walked here from Kathy's.'

'We'll take mine, then.'

'Where are we going?'

'Pilcox Cottage. When I was questioning him on Tuesday, North told me he was spending the weekend with the Haben-howe twins. I want to know what he was doing tonight.'

'I don't follow.'

'Worseley tried to ring me after he left on Friday. He told the station he'd remembered something that might identify the man we were interested in, and he'd ring again. And now he's dead. I don't like coincidences.'

'But there's nothing to link North with his death!' Scobie said incredulously.

'Suppose Worseley worked out that Trudy told Roger North he'd made her pregnant, and North discovered Worseley was about to tell us.'

'That's stretching things a bit,' Scobie said doubtfully. 'Shouldn't we wait for the PM and forensic?'

'The PM isn't likely to tell us much. He was burnt to a cinder according to the fire officer. And forensic could take days to report. I want to tackle North now.'

'It's five o'clock in the morning!'

'Which is a good time to question a suspect, Norris,' said Millson.

It was an hour after sunrise and the June sky was pale blue and cloudless when Millson parked outside Pilcox Cottage. Their footsteps echoed loudly in the early-morning quiet as they walked up the concrete path to the front door. Halfway there, Millson noticed the open door of the garage, and made a detour to it across the grass.

Stepping inside, he gazed around. Most of the space was taken up by the bronze Saab sports car. Scobie tapped him on the shoulder and pointed. Leaning against the rear wall were two racing bikes with crash helmets hanging by their straps from the handlebars.

Millson nodded and moved forward. He pointed to the bottle-clips in front of the handlebars.

'Two bottles of petrol would be enough, Norris.'

There was a sound behind them. Scobie whirled round. The tall figure of Hughie was silhouetted against the light, moving towards them menacingly.

'Leave this to me, George,' Scobie said quietly, 'he's a bit backward.' Speaking slowly and distinctly, he called out, 'It's all right, Hughie. We – are – policemen.'

'Whatdya want?' Hughie Cole finished buttoning up the old raincoat he'd put on over his pyjamas.

'We'd like to speak to Roger.'

'Rodge is in the 'ouse,' said Hughie. 'The door's this way.'

'Hang on a minute,' Millson said. Speaking carefully, as Scobie had done, he asked, 'Who rides these bikes, Hughie?'

'G and G. They's the' – Hughie paused to make sure he had the words right – 'county – ladies' – joint champions,' he said, speaking slowly and carefully. 'They come in together, see?'

'Do you ever ride them?'

'Nah, can't get the hang of the gears. I jus' keeps 'em clean.'

'The wheels on this one aren't too clean,' said Millson, pointing.

Hughie stooped forward and peered, a frown spreading over his face. 'Must've missed 'em, then.'

Millson nodded. 'OK. Show us to the front door.'

At the door, Hughie raised his hand to knock, then paused. 'They'll be sleeping,' he said.

'Wake them up, then,' Millson said impatiently.

Hughie turned. He was half a head taller than Scobie, and when he bent forward, in what seemed an aggressive movement, they instinctively stepped back.

'Wass your names?' Hughie asked, lowering his face to Millson's level.

'DCI Millson and DS Scobie,' said Millson.

Hughie looked at him blankly for a moment then turned back to the door. Pounding the solid oak panels with the flat of a large hand, he lifted the letterbox flap with the other hand and bawled through it, 'WAKE UP! Two coppers is 'ere!'

A moment later, an upstairs window opened and two chestnut heads craned out. Scobie smiled and gave them a wave. The heads withdrew and after an interval the bolts on the door were drawn and it opened. Georgina and Georgette stood framed in the doorway wearing pink satin pyjamas, and looking like sleepy-eyed children. Millson wondered why girls always seemed younger and smaller in their night-clothes.

He apologized for disturbing them and explained it was Roger North he wanted to speak to. They nodded gravely and invited him in. Behind them, Hughie Cole turned away and padded back to his caravan.

Seated in comfortable armchairs in the lounge, Millson and Scobie accepted an offer of coffee and one of the girls went to the kitchen while the other went upstairs to call Roger North.

When North came down a while later fully dressed in jacket, sports shirt and slacks, Millson and Scobie had drunk their coffee and Millson had finished the plateful of biscuits. He was missing his early-morning cigarette more than usual.

North sat down next to the Habenhowe twins on the sofa. They were still in their pyjamas, and apparently intending to remain there. Scobie suggested they might like to put some clothes on while the chief inspector interviewed Mr North.

They stood up. 'Don't let them bully you, Biggy,' said one.

'And you can ask for a solicitor,' said the other.

'Not yet, you can't,' Millson growled at an apprehensive-looking Roger North as they left the room. 'Where were you between one o'clock and two-thirty this morning, Mr North?'

'Here, of course. Why?'

'I'll come to that. Doing what?'

Roger North looked over his shoulder to the door then shrugged and said, 'If you really want to know, Chief Inspector, I was in bed with' – he hesitated momentarily – 'Georgette.' He smiled sheepishly. 'Doing what comes naturally.' His smile vanished when Scobie began writing. 'I wish you'd tell me what this is about.'

'All in good time,' Millson said. 'Do you ride a bike?'

'I can, but I don't own one.'

'What about the ones out there in the garage?'

'They're Georgina's and Georgette's.'

'Did you borrow one last night?'

'No.'

'Do you know Frank Worseley?'

'Yes, I know him. He's a builder down the hill here in Tanniford.'

'When did you last speak to him?'

'I haven't spoken to him since he put in a new front door for me about three months ago. Why? Has something happened to him?' There was an undertone of anxiety in his voice.

'Do you expect something to have happened to him, Mr North?'

'No-o. But since you keep asking me questions about him I presume something has.'

'Oh, it has indeed,' said Millson. 'Someone set fire to his place early this morning and burnt him to death.'

North's eyes flew wide. He gulped and stared at Millson. 'Why have you been asking *me* all these questions?'

'Because someone was seen riding away on a bike in this direction.'

'You surely don't think it was me? Why would I kill him? I hardly know him.' There was a quaver of fear in his voice now.

'Because he was about to inform us Trudy Thornton told *you* you were responsible for her pregnancy.'

North said wildly, 'That's ridiculous! You're accusing me of two murders now! And you haven't a shred of evidence against me for either of them.'

'And you haven't a credible alibi for either of them,' Millson retorted. 'These Habenhowe girls don't impress me in the least. We've made more enquiries and issued further appeals for your mystery taxi driver, and he hasn't come forward. That's because he doesn't exist, Mr North. You didn't take a taxi to Tanniford that night. You drove down here in your car and intercepted Trudy at Kelvedon station. Then you drove her to a lane near her home and killed her.'

'NO!' The single word burst from Roger North's lips in a shout, and his face began working agitatedly.

Millson watched impassively, waiting for whatever was

112

troubling him to come out. North took a deep breath and sat upright.

'I want to tell you the truth about that night, Chief Inspector.'

Scobie caught Millson's nod. Leaning forward, he said in a formal voice, 'Roger North, you do not have to say anything. But it may harm your defence if you do not mention, when questioned, something which you later rely on in court. Anything you do say may be given in evidence.'

'I understand,' North said quietly. He faced Millson. 'I didn't take a taxi from Colchester station. I was met by Mrs Howard and *she* drove me to Tanniford. We spent the night together at my house.'

Millson stared at him. 'Are you telling me you and Mrs Howard are lovers?' he asked incredulously.

'Yes. We have been for about six months.'

'Why didn't you tell us this before?'.

'Because of her husband. Charles would crucify us if he found out. I beg you to be discreet, Chief Inspector, when you ask Laura – Mrs Howard – about this. She'd be devastated if anything happened to her marriage.' He saw Millson's eyebrows rise. 'I . . . I was just a diversion, really.'

'Mrs Howard had better verify your story,' Millson said grimly. 'Or we'll have you in the nick faster than Concorde.'

'Oh, she will,' Roger North said confidently. Laura owed him that, at least. 'I hope you'll ask her today while Charles is out of the way in Brussels.' It wouldn't be his fault if the police found her with her new lover.

'Now, tell me why the Habenhowe girls said you spent the night with them?'

'They were trying to help me. They knew I'd spent the night with Laura and couldn't tell you.'

Scobie stirred restlessly in his seat. This didn't accord with Kathy's opinion of Georgina and Georgette at all. 'According to our information there isn't much affection between you and the twins,' he said. 'Why should they help you?'

'Because they knew I was innocent.' North gave a half-hearted laugh. 'Even they wouldn't want to see me charged with a murder I didn't commit.'

Scobie thought he didn't sound very convinced about it.

'It's incredible . . . him and Laura Howard,' Scobie said, fastening his seat belt. 'I know she's dishy, but she's years older than him.'

'Haven't *you* ever fancied an older woman, Norris?'

'No, I haven't as a matter of fact.'

'Ah well, there's time yet. You're still young,' Millson said impishly, starting the engine.

'I take it we're off to The Lawns?'

Millson nodded. 'I'd have liked breakfast first, though,' he said sorrowfully.

'Kathy will make us some.'

Millson's face brightened. 'Are you sure?' But he was already turning the car round.

It was nine o'clock when they arrived at The Lawns.

'My husband isn't here,' Laura Howard said as she opened the door. Her blonde hair hung loose around her shoulders and she was wearing a filmy negligée with very little beneath, as far as Scobie could see. Her appearance contrasted sharply with the childish innocence of the twins, he thought. Though, according to Kathy, the twins were anything but innocent, so perhaps Laura Howard in her turn was not as sensuous and abandoned as she looked.

'It's you we've come to see,' Millson told her.

Her eyes flashed briefly and then she said lightly, 'Goodness, why do you want to see me?'

'Perhaps we could come in?' Millson suggested.

'Yes, I suppose so.' She drew the negligée more closely about her.

'I don't mind waiting while you dress,' Millson said, as they entered the hall.

She shook her head. 'I've just run my bath. This won't take long, will it?'

'Probably not. I'll come straight to the point, Mrs Howard,'

Millson said. 'Mr North has just told us that the night Trudy Thornton was murdered you met him off his train at Colchester then drove to his house in Tanniford and spent the night together. Is that true?'

Her eyes widened slightly. 'Yes, it is,' she said calmly.

'You're lovers?'

'Well, it wasn't a one-night stand,' she said tartly.

Millson was perplexed. He'd expected reluctance . . . excuses . . . even denial, perhaps. Not this blunt admission.

'Is that all, Inspector?' She arched her eyebrows at him.

'Er . . . yes. Thank you for being so frank, Mrs Howard. We shall treat the information with discretion.'

'So I should hope,' she said. 'It has nothing whatever to do with your murder case.'

Dena was out when Millson returned home. A note beside his own on the kitchen table said she had gone for a swim at the leisure centre. There was a PS to it: *You promised to check that woman's references.* Dena persisted in calling Victoria Gill 'that woman'.

Millson sighed. He'd promised almost a week ago. Dena was right. He shouldn't allow a strange woman the run of the house without checking her credentials.

Opening his bureau desk, he retrieved the references Victoria Gill had supplied with her application, and picked up the telephone.

When Dena bounced into the house half an hour later, her dark hair in rats' tails and smelling of chlorine, she found him still sitting by the telephone, looking thoughtful.

'Did you see my note, Dad?'

'I did.'

His flat tone alerted her. She looked at his face. 'She's a crook, isn't she?' Her voice rose triumphantly. 'I knew it! What's she done?'

'Victoria Gill hasn't *done* anything, Dena. She's simply omitted to tell me something about herself.'

One of the households where Victoria Gill was working

knew her well. 'I've known Vicki for years,' the woman said on the phone, 'ever since her divorce . . .'

Millson wondered why Victoria Gill hadn't told him she was Charles Howard's ex-wife.

CHAPTER 13

On Monday morning, with Roger North no longer a suspect for the murder of Frank Worseley, Millson dispatched his officers to question the male associates of the women Worseley was reported to have attacked. He still suspected Worseley's death was connected in some way with Trudy Thornton's murder, but there was also a strong possibility he'd been killed by the vengeful husband or boyfriend of one of Worseley's victims.

In the middle of the morning Millson returned home. During the week and a half since he'd engaged Victoria Gill, his communication with her had been by means of notes left with her money on the hall table. Yesterday afternoon's revelation had to be handled face to face, though.

She was cleaning the oven in the kitchen. Her blonde hair was tucked beneath a head-band and she wore a blue boiler suit and rubber gloves.

'This is a surprise, Mr Millson,' she said with a smile as he came in through the back door.

'Why didn't you tell me you were once married to Charles Howard, Miss Gill?' he asked bluntly.

Her smile vanished and her mouth dropped in astonishment. Recovering, she threw down the cleaning-pad she was using and said sharply, 'Why should I? I divorced him eight years ago.'

'But you knew I was investigating the murder of his secretary, Trudy Thornton.'

'No, I didn't!' she said angrily. 'I had no idea until I saw you on television the other evening. I was going to mention it to you sometime and I resent being spoken to as though I've done something wrong.'

She tore off her head-band and tossed it on the table.

'D'you know why I started cleaning houses? It was the only work I could do that would fit round Gavin's school times. I was nineteen when I married. My son was born the next year and when I divorced Charles I hadn't worked for twelve years. I had no capital, just a rented flat. Charles paid maintenance for Gavin, but I had to support myself. And now I own a business. I built it from nothing. Nothing! So, don't you talk to me as though I'm some criminal!'

Taken aback by the fury of her outburst, Millson said contritely, 'I'm sorry. I didn't mean to upset you.' Her eyes still blazed at him. 'I really am sorry.' Slowly, the anger in her eyes died down and her mouth relaxed. Tentatively, he went on, 'Trudy became your husband's secretary before you were divorced so, presumably, you knew her.'

'Oh, yes . . . I knew Trudy,' Victoria Gill said bitterly. She peeled off the rubber gloves and dropped them in the sink. 'She was the reason I went ahead with the divorce. I might have waited to see if he got over Laura, but when he told me what he'd been up to with Trudy for years, that was the last straw.'

'Do you mean your husband was having an affair with her?'

'An affair?' Victoria Gill's voice rose derisively. 'She'd been his mistress for years. Charles slept with her every time they were away at conferences together. He told me so when he asked for a divorce so he could marry Laura. He said Trudy didn't mean anything, though. It was simply that he hated sleeping alone, and took her to bed for comfort.' She giggled. 'I said, "You mean like a hot-water bottle?". He was ever so cross.' She giggled again.

'I see.' Millson digested the information. 'It's probably unfair to ask you, Miss Gill, but –'

'*Vicki*,' she said firmly. 'Ask away.'

'Vicki, then. Do you think he continued his relationship with Trudy after he remarried?'

She screwed up her mouth. 'I doubt it, considering how badly he wanted Laura. She had him well and truly hooked.'

Had his infatuation lasted, though? Millson wondered.

Laura Howard's brazen admission of adultery suggested otherwise.

Victoria Gill apparently had doubts too, because she went on, 'Mind you, today . . . eight years on' – her eyes crinkled at the corners – 'Charles might need a hottie again. And I expect the ever-loyal Trudy was still willing to warm his bed for him.' She noticed Millson's interested expression. 'Why? Does it matter?'

'It might. Trudy was pregnant.'

'Ah, but it wouldn't be Charles,' she said promptly. 'She was too careful for that. Charles would have done his nut if she'd landed him with a baby. Think of the scandal.'

Precisely, Millson thought. Question was, did Howard commit murder to prevent it.

'I think Trudy told Charles Howard the baby was his,' Millson said, as he relayed Victoria Gill's information to Scobie over beer and sandwiches in the Red Lion. 'And *that's* what Worseley was going to tell us.'

'And Howard killed her?'

'It's possible. It's like the Glasgow case I told you about. A pregnant mistress run over by her lover and made to look like a hit-and-run fatality. How long do you reckon it would take him to drive to Kelvedon from his flat in London?'

'He'd do it comfortably in an hour at that time of night.'

Millson nodded. 'That's what I thought. Find out if he's back from Brussels.'

Charles Howard made no attempt to hide his annoyance that evening as he took them into the study and sat down at his desk. 'I hope this is important, Chief Inspector. I've had a tiring weekend and I'm looking forward to a restful evening with my wife.'

'We wouldn't be here at all if you hadn't misled us over your relationship with the dead woman, Mr Howard,' Millson said harshly. 'Or perhaps you thought it was all right to be economical with the truth.'

There was no change in Charles Howard's expression, but

Scobie noticed his body stiffen in the chair. 'In what way have I misled you?'

'You implied you knew nothing about Trudy's private life. But in fact, you once had an intimate relationship with her.'

'You're saying I slept with my secretary?' Charles Howard's tone was acid. 'You realize the seriousness of that accusation to someone in my position?'

'Yes, I do.'

'I presume you have a source for this offensive allegation?'

'Yes . . . your ex-wife.' That rattled him, Millson noted with satisfaction, as Charles Howard's eyes flared with shock.

Recovering, Howard said, 'Victoria is just being spiteful. She's lying.'

'She says you admitted your relationship with Trudy at the time of the divorce.'

Charles Howard gave a slight smile and appeared to relax. 'I invented an affair with Trudy to persuade Victoria our marriage had broken down. I was in love with Laura, and I wanted a divorce so that I could marry her.'

'I see, sir,' Millson said heavily. 'So what you're saying is that *you* were lying when you told your ex-wife you were sleeping with your secretary. Which means your ex-wife is *not* lying, of course.'

Scobie looked up from his notes and hoped George Millson knew what he was doing. Charles Howard was clearly furious at the criticism.

'Perhaps you'll explain what this intrusion into my private affairs has to do with your murder investigation, Millson,' Howard said through tight lips. 'There had better be a good reason for it. I warned you before, I might speak to your Chief Constable. This time I certainly will.'

'Very well, Mr Howard, I'll speak plainly. Your secretary was pregnant. Your ex-wife says the woman had been your mistress for years and you couldn't have stood the scandal if she'd had a baby. And the woman has been murdered.'

'In other words, you mean I killed her,' Howard said sharply.

'It's a possibility, sir,' Millson said equably. 'Which means I have a duty to ask whatever questions I think necessary to

120

eliminate you from our enquiries. So, if you wouldn't mind, I'd like you to go over your movements on the night of the murder again.'

Charles Howard sighed impatiently. 'Very well. As I told you, I was waiting upon the Minister that night, and it was late when I left the Commons. I went by Underground from Westminster to Victoria, and from there I walked to my flat and went to bed.'

'How late is late, sir?' Scobie asked.

Howard's face swivelled towards him. 'I don't know – about eleven-thirty, I think.'

'And what time did you reach your flat?'

'It would have been about twenty minutes later, I suppose.'

'And the address?'

Howard gave an address near Eccleston Square.

'And where was your car?' Scobie asked, busily writing. 'You told us you drove to Sunningdale for a meeting in the morning and then drove on to London.'

For a moment Howard seemed uncertain. Then he said, 'It was parked outside my flat. I have a resident's parking space.'

'Colour and make, please?' Scobie asked.

'It's a black BMW.'

'Thank you.' Scobie nodded to Millson to indicate he'd finished.

'A final question, sir,' Millson said. 'You told us before that there was no one to confirm your movements after you left the House of Commons. Is that still the case?'

'Yes.' Howard spat the word out.

'I want you to check his story, Norris,' Millson said as he nosed his car cautiously from the drive and on to the road. 'Liaise with the Met if you have to. If his car was outside the flat as he says, someone should have seen it.'

A wave of nostalgia swept over Scobie when he emerged from the Underground at Victoria the following morning. Before he transferred to the Essex police four years ago he'd served with the Metropolitan Force. The Victoria area was well known to him although, strolling along Buckingham Palace Road to Eccleston Square, he noticed that it had changed a lot in four years.

He sometimes wondered if he should have stayed with the Met. He missed London's bustling energy . . . the urgency . . . everyone hurrying. And being at the centre of things. But there had been a downside . . . areas of squalor . . . druggies . . . people sleeping rough. And if he hadn't moved to north Essex, he wouldn't have met Kathy.

Norris Scobie was very happy with Kathy. They'd met three years ago when he was working on a kidnapping case. He'd fallen for the willowy, auburn-haired girl almost at once and, if he'd had his way, they would have been married by now. Kathy had other ideas, though. She'd seen friends rush into marriage and part again a year or so later.

'Let's live together,' she suggested, 'and see how we get on.'

He'd settled for that. No, he thought, he wasn't at all sorry he'd left London.

He located the address Charles Howard had given. It was in one of Pimlico's streets of grandiose Georgian houses. He mounted the steps to the white portico and pressed the button on the entryphone marked 'caretaker'. After he'd pressed it several times, a voice from the basement area called, 'Down here!'

Returning to the pavement, Scobie pushed open a small iron gate and descended some steps to the basement. The caretaker, a middle-aged man in a waistcoat, stood in a narrow doorway underneath the portico. Scobie showed his warrant card and was invited into the basement flat.

Millson was donning his jacket and about to leave the office for a late lunch, when Scobie phoned.

The caretaker, who had a worm's eye view of street level from his basement window, had seen Charles Howard return to his flat at about ten-thirty on the night of the murder, Scobie told Millson. 'That's earlier than Howard said,' Millson commented.

'Yes, and what's more,' Scobie said, sounding jubilant, 'he went out again soon after. *In his car*. And he hadn't returned when the caretaker went to bed at one o'clock.'

'We've got him, then,' Millson said. 'Get back here as soon as you can and we'll nail him.'

While Scobie was on his way back from London, Millson called on Trudy Thornton's mother in Sible Hedingham. He hoped she could confirm Charles Howard's intimate relationship with her daughter.

He found Joyce Thornton in an indignant mood. Earlier that day the coroner's office had told her Trudy's body could not be released for burial. Not without a second, independent postmortem . . . which she would have to pay for.

'It's not right, Mr Millson. That's my daughter they got there in the morgue. She belongs to me . . . I'm her next of kin.'

He'd explained the reason to her. That when a suspect was brought to trial, defence lawyers could request another, independent, postmortem to enable them to challenge the official one. If the victim had been buried, the body had to be exhumed. The only way to avoid that was to have an independent postmortem carried out before burial.

'I know how you feel, Mrs Thornton, but I'm afraid that's the way it is,' Millson said sympathetically.

She sniffed. 'Seems to me the victims and relatives get the rotten end of everything. What did you want to ask me?'

'How well did you know Trudy's boss, Charles Howard?'

'Not well at all,' she said. 'Only to say hello and goodbye to if I happened to be at her place when he brought her home.'

'Did Trudy talk about him?'

'Not a lot. She used to tell me about the places they went to . . . Paris . . . Strasbourg . . . Madrid . . . Mr Howard took her everywhere, you know. Said she was his right hand and he couldn't manage without her. She worked hard for him . . . taking notes, typing, making arrangements . . .'

'How do you think things were between them on a personal level?' Millson asked in a neutral tone.

123

Mrs Thornton looked at him from the corner of her eyes. 'Was she sleeping with him, you mean?' She didn't seem offended. 'Well, she used to joke she spent more time with him than his wife 'cos his wife only had him between dinner and breakfast, and she had him all day. And when they was away she had him nights as well. I never took it that way, though.' She shook her head doubtfully. 'If she *was* sleeping with him she never let on to me.' Her eyes slid into the corners again. 'Why you asking? D'you think it was him put her in the family way, then?'

Millson decided against telling her about Frank Worseley. 'No, but he may have thought he had.'

Millson was feeling disgruntled when he picked up Scobie at Colchester station that evening on their way to interview Charles Howard. Before leaving he'd thought it wise to let Superintendent Kitchen know that the man he suspected of murdering Trudy Thornton was an under secretary of state at the Home Office.

'I hope you're not thinking of arresting him on the strength of what you have so far, George,' the superintendent said.

'No,' Millson said huffily. 'But I might if his answers aren't satisfactory.'

The superintendent sucked in his cheeks, making hollows either side of his mouth. 'You'd better be damned sure of your case before you do that.'

Millson was also unhappy that Trudy's mother hadn't known of Howard's involvement with her daughter. He said as much to Scobie on the way to West Bergholt.

Scobie was not comforting. 'Funny that. If she *was* still his mistress you'd think her mother would know – even if they managed to hide it from everyone else,' he said.

'You think his ex-wife is wrong, then?'

'I think she could be,' Scobie said cautiously. 'And it was only her opinion . . . there was nothing to back it up.'

Millson was silent for a while. Then he said, 'They'd been at it a long time. Long-time lovers become skilful at conceal-ment. Either that, or they grow careless. And from what we know of these two, I'd say they were in the first category.'

124

Scobie wondered if he was speaking from personal experience. Millson had divorced his wife long before Scobie joined him, but Scobie gathered from his occasional comments that she'd cheated on him for a long time.

Charles Howard was cool and polite as he led them into the study. 'More questions, I presume, Chief Inspector?'

'One in particular, Mr Howard,' Millson said as he took a seat in one of the leather armchairs. 'Where did you go when you drove away from your flat at ten-thirty on the night Trudy Thornton was murdered?'

Howard picked up the letter-opener on his desk and fiddled with it. It bothered Millson that he showed no surprise and seemed untroubled by the question. 'I don't think that has anything to do with you,' Howard said quietly.

'And *I* don't think you realize the seriousness of your position,' Millson retorted.

'Really? Perhaps you'd be good enough to explain it to me, then,' Howard said calmly.

'Trudy was pregnant and your ex-wife says she had been your mistress for years and probably still was. Trudy was met at Kelvedon station at midnight by someone driving a large car. Someone she knew, because she wouldn't have entered a stranger's car in those circumstances. Your car is a big BMW, and a witness says you drove off from your flat at ten-thirty that night and hadn't returned at one o'clock when he went to bed. Yet when we were last here and I asked you to account for your movements that night, you told us you went home to your flat and went to bed. That wasn't true. So, where did you go?'

'Well, I didn't drive to Kelvedon and meet Trudy,' Howard said easily. 'I can put your mind at rest on that.' He opened a drawer in his desk and took out two sheets of paper. 'That' – he said, handing the first to Millson – 'is the invoice for servicing my car by the garage near my flat. It shows the car's mileage when they serviced it that afternoon. And this' – he passed the other document to Millson – 'is the MOT certificate issued by the test centre near Vauxhall Bridge where the car was taken for its MOT the next morning. You will notice the mileage was practically the same as when the garage serviced it. Which means I did *not* drive it to Kelvedon that night.'

Taken by surprise, Millson stared at the MOT certificate and the garage service sheet. The car's mileage on Wednesday afternoon and Thursday morning was virtually the same. He passed the documents to Scobie.

Scobie scrutinized them and said quickly, 'There *is* a difference of ten miles in the two figures, Mr Howard, and the test centre is only about half a mile from the garage. I know, because I used to patrol that area.'

'Indeed? Well, I expect the garage took the car for a road test.'

'For *ten miles*?' Scobie queried.

Howard ignored him and turned to Millson. 'There is no cause for you to concern yourself further with my private affairs, I think, Mr Millson.' He stood up.

Reluctantly, Millson came to his feet. Howard had not explained where he went that night or why he lied about it. However, in the face of an apparently solid alibi, he had no excuse for questioning him further.

Grudgingly, he said, 'No, I have no more questions, Mr Howard, and thank you for your time.'

'He *knew* we'd ask him about the car!' Millson fumed as he snatched at his seat belt and snapped it on. 'Why the hell didn't he admit using it last time? Why wait until now to produce that alibi like a rabbit out of a hat?'

'Looks as though he didn't want to admit using it until he had to.'

'It's perverse,' Millson snarled as he turned his car round and headed down the drive from The Lawns. 'You know, Norris,' he went on, 'it requires a certain type of mind to reach the top echelon of the civil service. Intellectually arrogant . . . boringly logical.'

Scobie glanced sideways at him. Millson must be smarting badly under Charles Howard's rebuttal to carry on like this. He said helpfully, 'He could have turned back the mileage clock before he took it for the MOT. Or he could have picked up another car somewhere.'

'He could have done all sorts of things, Norris!' Millson said savagely. 'But we don't have any evidence of them, do we?'

Scobie said no more. He knew better than to try and cheer Millson up when he was in a mood.

A while later Millson muttered, 'You're right. He could have used another car. I want the car-hire firms within five miles of Howard's flat telephoned and asked for details of anyone who took out a vehicle between ten-thirty and eleven that night.'

CHAPTER 14

When he arrived home the following evening George Millson found his daughter standing on the kitchen table and Victoria Gill, her mouth full of pins, moving around her pinning the hem of her skirt.

'Vicki's helping me alter my skirt, Dad,' said Dena.

Vicki? Was the war over between them then? 'It's short enough already,' he said disapprovingly.

Victoria Gill removed the pins from her mouth. 'We're letting it *down*, Mr Millson.' She looked up at Dena. 'The hem's straight now, Dena. You can tack it ready for sewing.'

'Ta.' Dena put a hand on her father's shoulder and jumped down from the table. 'Vicki was here when I came home from school. Actually, she's waiting to see you,' she said, ogling him as she went out.

Victoria Gill smiled. 'I think she's forgiven me for invading her room. We're friends now.'

'I'm glad,' Millson said. 'Why did you want to see me?'

'It's about my ex-husband and Trudy. My son, Gavin, walked in on them at the Pimlico flat about a month ago. Caught them in flagrante delicto, as Charles was fond of putting it. We lesser mortals would say they were bonking. They were so busy at it they didn't notice Gavin, and he left smartly. It was lunchtime and he only went there to collect his cricket clothes. His father lets him store his sports gear in the flat while he's up at London University. It all came out yesterday when I asked Gavin when he was going to see his father again. He blew up and said never, and then told me what had happened.'

Millson had only one question. 'He was sure it was Trudy Thornton?'

128

'Oh yes. He'd met her often enough.'

'Thank you. You did right to tell me,' Millson said.

The telephone calls to car-hire firms within a five-mile radius of Howard's London flat had been unproductive, and Millson was uncertain of his ground as Scobie drove him to The Lawns later that evening. Howard had been in Brussels last weekend so he could not have killed Frank Worseley, and although he'd hidden his true relationship with Trudy, that didn't mean he'd murdered her. Of the three essentials: means, motive and opportunity, Howard had had the first two, but not the third. It was the lack of opportunity – being able to place him at the scene of crime – that hampered Millson. So far, Charles Howard had managed to avoid telling the truth without actually lying. Millson decided to use shock tactics to break through his guard this time.

Scobie had made the appointment for half past nine. The appetizing smell of a recent meal lingered in the hall as they followed Charles Howard across the hall to his study. He was stiffly polite as usual.

'What is it this time?' he asked as they seated themselves.

'I want to ask you about your relationship with Trudy, Mr Howard,' Millson said.

'Not that again,' Howard said petulantly. 'I told you, Chief Inspector, my ex-wife is an unreliable witness on that subject.'

Millson lobbed his grenade. 'What about your son?' He watched it explode and Howard's eyes spring wide open and stare at him from a shocked face.

'*Gavin?*'

Millson nodded. 'He saw you in the flat with Trudy one lunchtime about a month ago. What lawyers in divorce courts used to refer to as in flagrante delicto, I believe.'

'Oh, God.' Howard's face crumpled. He put his elbows on the desk and covered his face with his hands. A moment later he looked up and said fiercely, 'How dare you question my son about my private life!'

'This is a murder investigation and I'll question who I like

129

about what I like,' Millson retorted angrily. 'As it happens, though, I didn't question your son.'

'My ex-wife must have told you then. I expect she enjoys feeding you dirt like that.'

'Instead of criticizing other people for telling the truth, I advise you to start using it yourself,' Millson said sternly. 'You have persistently evaded it and wasted my time. We'll continue this at the station.' He stood up.

'Oh God, no.' Howard sagged in his chair, his face ashen. 'It isn't necessary, Chief Inspector. I'll tell you anything you want to know. Please . . . you must understand my position.' He leaned forward, pleading. 'I have to attend an important conference in New York this weekend. I'm due to fly out tomorrow. If the press get a whiff of this, there will be scurrilous headlines and . . .' He caught his breath. 'I'll be finished.'

'Is that why you killed her?' Millson asked. 'To avoid the scandal?'

'I did *not* kill her! I was fond of her, for heaven's sake! I know absolutely nothing about her murder. I misled you about my relationship with her solely to protect my wife and me from the scandal. There was no other reason.'

Scobie heard Millson grunt. Scobie had learned to interpret Millson's grunts. The tone indicated sympathy, a change of subject, scepticism, or just a clearing of the throat. This grunt was distinctly sceptical and, for the first time, Scobie felt sympathy for Charles Howard. This aloof, fastidious man had been cuckolded by a jobbing builder and his private secretary, and now George Millson was going to haul him off to the police station in ignominy.

Millson sat down again, however. Folding his hands over his abdomen, he said, 'Very well. The truth, then. The whole truth this time.'

Howard's face lit up with relief and he nodded. Speaking unemotionally, he explained that Trudy had become his mistress shortly after she became his secretary twelve years ago. The affair had stopped when his first wife divorced him and he married Laura. Then, last year, it had started again.

'You know what it's like away from home ... feeling lonely ... needing warmth,' he said.

Millson nodded. *Needing his hottie*, Victoria Gill had called it.

'Seven-year itch too, I suppose,' Howard said wryly. 'Laura and I had been married seven years.'

The relationship had not affected his marriage, he insisted. He and his wife had a good marriage. Then a month ago, out of the blue, Trudy told him she was pregnant.

Howard drew a shuddering breath. 'It was a dreadful blow. But we discussed it sensibly. I was prepared to support Trudy and the child, and Trudy was as anxious as I was to keep the matter quiet.'

'And keep it from your wife?' Millson asked.

'No, certainly not. I confessed to Laura immediately. She was very good about it ... very understanding. Provided I ended the affair at once – which, of course, I did – and Trudy was discreet, she was willing to accept the situation. And that's how things stood when this terrible thing happened to Trudy.'

Millson studied him. Howard returned his gaze for a moment, then dropped his eyes. Shame? Guilt? The story was plausible enough, and so was his manner. There was still the matter of the unexplained mileage on his car, however.

'Let's return to your movements on the night of the murder,' Millson said. 'You produced some very neat proof of the mileage on your car as evidence you couldn't have driven to Kelvedon. But there were ten miles unaccounted for.'

Howard frowned. 'I don't see why that matters now.'

'It matters, Mr Howard, because you could have driven to the outskirts of London and picked up a hired car to use instead of your own.'

Howard looked alarmed. 'But I've told you I didn't drive down there!'

'You've told me lots of things,' Millson said tartly, 'and some of them were lies.'

'I have explained why that was.'

'So now explain those extra miles,' Millson said. 'And don't

131

suggest the garage took it for a long road test. They didn't. We've checked.'

Howard shrugged. 'I just went for a drive around.' He saw Millson's sceptical expression. 'Along the Embankment,' he added. 'I'd had a worrying evening in the official box and I needed to relax.'

Millson regarded him for a while, his face showing disbelief. 'Very well,' he said, coming to his feet. 'Our enquiries into that will continue.' He noticed Howard's eyes cloud with worry. 'Meantime, I'd like to confirm what you've said about Trudy with your wife.'

'Is that really necessary?'

'Yes, it is,' Millson said firmly.

Howard hesitated then rose from his seat. 'She's in the lounge. Come with me, please.'

Laura Howard was sitting reading a magazine by the open French windows where the cool evening air drifted in from the patio. She wore a navy-blue top and white shorts, and her long legs were stretched out in front of her. Scobie admired them covertly. They were as shapely as Kathy's.

Howard said, 'The Chief Inspector would like a word with you, darling.'

'Of course.' She smiled and waved at nearby chairs.

Millson waited for Charles Howard to leave before he sat down.

'I understand your husband told you of his relationship with Trudy Thornton, Mrs Howard.'

'Yes, he told me everything.'

'It must have been a great shock to you.'

She drew in her legs and sat up in the chair. 'A shock, yes, but it wasn't the end of the world.'

'You didn't mind that he would help her financially . . . support the child and so on?'

'Mind? Of course I minded! It was the only thing to be done, though, and I accepted the situation. That was provided she went away to have the child and kept quiet about it.'

'And Trudy agreed to that?'

'So Charles tells me.'

132

'You didn't discuss it with her yourself?'

'Certainly not! Any more than I'd do my husband's dirty washing. Whatever next!' Laura Howard snorted.

'Just for the record, Mrs Howard, where were you at the time Trudy Thornton was killed?'

Her eyes never wavered. She glanced over her shoulder to the doorway and lowered her voice. 'You *know* where I was, Chief Inspector. I was with Roger. I met him off the train and we spent the night at his place.'

'What time did you leave here?' Millson asked.

'About one o'clock, I should think. His train arrived at twenty-past, if I remember correctly.'

'And what kind of car do you drive, please?'

'A blue Ford Mondeo.'

'Thank you,' Millson said.

Millson was silent as Scobie drove him home. He was depressed. He now didn't have a suspect for Trudy's murder, nor for Worseley's. Perhaps his whole investigation had been flawed. He stirred restlessly as Scobie turned on to the Avenue of Remembrance.

'He went *somewhere*,' he muttered.

'What?' Scobie inclined his head.

'Howard. He went somewhere. He didn't go for a drive along the Embankment. Fat lot of relaxation that would be. He's lying again and I can't think why.'

Scobie could. He wasn't going to tell Millson, though. Not until he'd rung one of his old cronies in the Met.

CHAPTER 15

The following morning Millson received the postmortem report on Frank Worseley. There were no wounds on his body, and no injuries other than those attributable to the fire. The body had been badly burned, but it had been possible to carry out an analysis of the blood and the stomach contents. This revealed that Worseley had consumed a large quantity of alcohol shortly before death.

The report by the forensic team arrived on Millson's desk an hour later. There was no doubt the fire had been started deliberately. Evidence of petrol had been found in the bedroom, on the landing outside and on the stairs down to the front door. The fragments of two drinking glasses had been discovered in the debris in the bedroom. The pieces of glass were contaminated with carbon deposit and it was impossible to lift fingerprints from them. A fragment from one of the rims had traces of lipstick on it.

Millson frowned. There had been a woman in Worseley's bedroom that evening. Who was she? He delved in the side drawer of his desk for the bag of barley sugars he kept there and put two lumps in his mouth at once.

Perhaps the cyclist seen leaving the scene had been a woman. Until now he'd thought of a man exacting revenge on Worseley. Why not a woman, though? A mother or sister of one of his victims. Or the victim herself. A wife in the United States had cut off her husband's penis after he raped her. Worseley should have been thankful to die with his manhood intact, Millson thought malignantly.

He rolled the barley sugars around his mouth with his tongue. You needed to hate a man pretty badly to burn him to death in his bed. So, revenge was the most likely motive for Worseley's murder. But there was the coincidence of him being killed when he'd been on the point of revealing something about Trudy Thornton.

Millson disliked coincidences. They disturbed the pattern of things. They led one to look for significance in them when there was none and they were simply coincidences. However, until he knew what it was Worseley had been going to tell him, the suspicion his murder had not been a coincidence, and was connected with Trudy's murder, would remain.

At the moment, it was imperative to find the woman who had been in Worseley's bedroom that evening. Millson went along to the incident room to brief his team and instruct the press officer to make an appeal through the media for the woman to come forward.

Roger North's lunch that day was a hurried sandwich and coffee in a sandwich bar in Tothill Street. He had an hour to prepare a revised brief for Howard before this afternoon's meeting with the Chief Constables.

The morning's meeting on hiving off the Police National Computer to an agency had been disastrous. Charles Howard had not been his usual alert self and Roger had listened in disbelief as he misinterpreted a vital point in the brief Roger had provided for him. Charles seemed preoccupied. Roger would have suspected he'd become aware of Laura's new lover if her phone call on Sunday night hadn't implied she didn't have one.

She had phoned him in Finchley soon after his return from Tanniford, and upbraided him for informing the police of their affair. 'How do you think I felt, having to outface that brute of a police inspector?' she demanded. 'I was mortified.'

'Laura, they were going to arrest me for Trudy's murder!'

'Why on earth should they think *you* killed her?'

'They believed I'd made her pregnant, and didn't want her and a baby round my neck. They even thought I killed Worseley, because he was about to inform on me.'

'But that's absurd!'

'I know. But as they couldn't find the taxi I told them I took from Colchester, they were convinced I drove down to

Kelvedon, met Trudy off her train and killed her. I *had* to tell them about being with you. I was being accused of murder, for God's sake!'

'It's all right,' she said soothingly. 'I understand, and I forgive you.' Her tone had become warmer.

'Will I see you again, Laura?'

'Of course you will, poppet. But we have to be careful. Be patient, darling.'

Roger was cheerful on his way home that evening. The afternoon meeting had gone well, Laura still wanted him, and he was finished with Georgina and Georgette. Free of the threat they had held over him since they turned up at his house on the Saturday after Trudy's murder.

That was the first contact he'd had with them since their sixteenth birthday party and he'd been alarmed by their sudden intrusion that day. Before he could discover what they wanted, the police arrived. Georgina and Georgette had seemed intent on staying, and he'd only persuaded them to leave by promising to meet them later.

In the Black Dog that evening they told him they knew everything about his affair with Laura. Every visit she made to his house . . . the time she arrived . . . the time she left. The information had been logged and was utterly reliable, they explained. Roger realized then that their informant was his next-door neighbour, Joe Sparrow. Joe Sparrow – who lived alone, and enjoyed spying on people.

At one time, Sparrow had owned the butcher's shop in the High Street. As a sideline – and contrary to hygiene regulations – he supplied village children with ice-lollies and ice-creams from a cold chest at the rear of the shop. As a child, Roger's mother had forbidden him ever to enter Joe Sparrow's shop. When he was older, and asked her about it, she hinted darkly that some children came out of the shop with more than an ice-lolly in their hand. They had money as well – more money than they went in with.

The young Georgina and Georgette were frequently in the shop. Some in the village thought Joe Sparrow had a soft spot for them and their widowed mother. Certainly Gladys seemed to receive the best cuts of meat, and the twins always had plenty of pocket money. However, there were others who believed Georgina and Georgette were blackmailing Joe Sparrow over what went on in the back of his shop.

Whatever the relationship had been then between them and Joe Sparrow, a link had continued to the present day, and he was occasionally seen calling at Pilcox Cottage. Rumour had it that Georgina and Georgette encouraged his visits and supplied him with bottles of whisky in return for tittle-tattle about Tanniford.

Roger was appalled to learn of the use they had made of Sparrow's information about him and Laura. They had taken the trouble to find out Laura's address, trace her husband, and identify his position at the Home Office.

'He's a very important guy, Roger,' said Georgina, taking a sip of her rum and Coke. 'Well, you know that, of course, because you work for him.'

'It's very naughty of you, screwing the boss's wife, Roger,' said Georgette. 'Very naughty indeed.'

'I wonder what Mr Howard would do if we told him,' Georgina said casually.

A cold fear gripped Roger North as more ugly words flowed from their pretty mouths. Charles would destroy him . . . and Laura. It would be the end of her marriage . . . her happiness . . . She'd be devastated. He couldn't let it happen.

'Why are you doing this to me?' he asked. 'Why do you hate me?'

'We don't hate you, Biggy. Quite the opposite, in fact,' said Georgette.

'We just wanted you to know your secret is safe with us, that's all,' said Georgina.

That was all they would say . . . then. But he knew they wouldn't have gone to these lengths without a reason. There had to be something they wanted from him. He learned what it was the night they took him to the Chinese restaurant.

They had been in a kittenish mood. Especially Georgette. Roger found he could still tell Georgette from Georgina when she turned her eyes on him.

'The thing is, Biggy . . .' Georgette paused and smiled

across the table at him. 'We want a child. And we don't want any Tom, Dick or Harry for the father. We want a Roger and —' She broke off. 'Oh, do close your mouth, Biggy, or everyone will think you're gaga.'

Georgina said earnestly, 'We've thought it out carefully. We shall never marry or take a partner, and there's no one we know as well as you, or who's as suitable.'

'You have the brains and we have the looks,' said Georgette. 'Between us we shall produce two wonderful children.'

'*Two*! You mean you expect me to . . . *Both* of you?'

'Of course,' Georgina said crisply. 'Georgie and I do everything together, you know we do.'

'You can manage that, can't you, Biggy?' asked Georgette.

He searched their faces, unable to believe they were serious. Then the fear and tension that had built up in him as he listened to their crazy proposal suddenly erupted.

'No! You're mad! I won't do it.'

Their mood changed like a curtain dropping. 'Should we address the letter "C. Howard Esquire" or "Charles Howard CB"?' Georgette asked her sister. She turned to Roger. 'He is a CB, isn't he, Biggy?'

'We'll post the letter tonight,' said Georgina. 'Did you know we had photographs as well?'

Roger stared at them like a rabbit transfixed in headlights. Unless he satisfied their stupid whim this crazy pair would wreck his career and Laura's marriage.

'All right,' he muttered. 'I'll do it. But the whole thing is preposterous. What happens afterwards when the pair of you start waddling around with fat tums? What will people say?'

'Don't worry about that,' said Georgette. 'No one will know you're the father.'

'And no one will believe you if you say you are,' said Georgina, 'because we shall deny it. We can't have you interfering with our plans.'

Plans? Roger looked around the restaurant. Everyone else seemed normal. He wasn't in a dream . . . he was in the company of two nutcases. People had always said the Habenhowe twins were insane. He believed it now. Maybe they even planned to . . . An hysterical giggle escaped him before he could control it.

'Are you all right, Biggy?' asked Georgette.

He nodded, not trusting himself to speak. He'd remembered that certain female spiders *killed* their partner after he'd mated with them.

His memory of the rest of the evening had been hazy. He recalled drinking a lot. He also recalled asking when he was required to perform, and being told it had to be next weekend because that was the middle of their fertile period.

Now, in retrospect, he wasn't sure he believed a word they'd said. Not after the death of that man Worseley and being very nearly arrested for his murder. So far as he knew, there was no connection between the twins and Worseley. Yet he had a nagging fear that his death, and his own presence at the cottage that weekend, had not been a coincidence.

A day later, on Friday of that week, Millson acknowledged he was at a dead end on the Trudy Thornton murder. The investigation into Frank Worseley's death seemed to be heading the same way. The enquiries on car-hire firms had been extended to a wider area, but had not turned up anyone like Charles Howard hiring a vehicle in the hours preceding Trudy's murder. And the three women Worseley assaulted had been interviewed, as well as their friends and relatives – male and female – and had all given a satisfactory account of their movements on the night he was killed.

Sitting at his desk, Millson reviewed the investigations and his conduct of them. In the case of Trudy Thornton he'd assumed – and still believed – the motive for her murder had to do with her being pregnant. There had been four suspects: Alec Pethard, Roger North, Frank Worseley and Charles Howard. Pethard he'd excluded when Worseley confessed to making Trudy pregnant. North eventually produced the alibi that he'd spent the night of Trudy's murder with Laura Howard, and she had corroborated it. Worseley was ruled out because it was clear he'd been telling the truth about Trudy. She *had* blamed the baby on someone else: she had told Charles Howard the baby was his. And now Charles Howard had come up with an apparently unshakeable alibi.

Millson sighed. He was left with no suspects and no further leads. Up Shit Creek without a paddle, as his grandfather used to say.

Worseley's murder was more clear cut. He'd been killed in an arson attack and that pointed to the motive being hate or revenge. His victims had been eliminated from suspicion, along with their relatives and associates. That left the unknown woman in Worseley's bedroom before the fire started, and the cyclist seen leaving the scene just afterwards. Neither of them had come forward and they could be one and the same. The cyclist had sped off up Pilcox Hill towards Pilcox Cottage where the Habenhowe twins lived. There were two racing bikes in their garage and when he and Scobie interviewed North there a few hours after the fire, one of the bikes looked to have been used recently. The wheels were dirty, whereas the other bike was spotlessly clean.

Millson put another two barley sugars in his mouth and sucked them energetically. Coincidences? A woman in the bedroom . . . a cyclist who went like the wind up Pilcox Hill . . . racing bikes in the garage . . . and two girls who were county champions. *All* coincidences? Millson crunched the barley sugars into fragments. There were too damn many of them not to be significant. Swallowing the remains of the sweets he thumped on the partition wall for Scobie to come in from next door.

'I think the female in Worseley's bedroom and the cyclist going like the wind up Pilcox Hill could have been one of the Habenhowe girls, Norris,' he told a surprised-looking Scobie. 'They had the means and the opportunity to kill Worseley. What I need is a motive . . . some link between him and them. They've lived in Tanniford all their lives and so had he. Maybe there was some old grudge between them we don't know about – something serious enough to warrant their torching him. And if it was that serious, it could have come to our notice at the time. See what you can find in our local records.'

The sergeant in charge of the divisional records was less

than pleased with Scobie's request. A hand-search through card indices and archives to look for past references to Frank Worseley and Georgina and Georgette Habenhowe was a major undertaking.

'How far back d'you want us to go?'

Scobie shrugged. 'How long does a grudge last? Do the last five years to begin with.'

The sergeant's face brightened. 'Ah well, that's not so bad. We've done a back-record conversion on the last two. They're on computer now. The lad over there can search those for you right away.' He indicated a clerk sitting at a terminal on the far side of the room.

Scobie crossed to him and explained his quest. 'We've got a new information-retrieval system up and running that does just what you're asking for, Sarge,' said the clerk. 'What are the names?'

'Georgina and Georgette Habenhowe, and Frank Worseley.'

The clerk turned to the keyboard and keyed in the names. 'Have I spelt them correctly?'

Scobie peered at the screen and nodded.

'If there's a link between them – either directly, or indirectly through a third party – this system will find it,' the clerk said. He went on chattily, 'The system uses a tree architecture so the search hops from branch to branch instead of hunting sequentially along a string and –'

'Spare me the technical stuff and get on with it, will you,' Scobie said.

'Sorry, Sarge.' The clerk pressed some keys. A few seconds later he said, 'You're out of luck,' as *No link found* appeared on the screen.

A thought occurred to Scobie. 'One of your moments of inspiration, Norris,' Millson called it later. 'Try adding Hugh Cole to the list,' he told the clerk. 'Spelt C-O-L-E.'

'Right.' The clerk's fingers click-clacked the keys again. Almost at once the name 'Auriol French' appeared on the screen with a symbol alongside it.

'What does that mean?' Scobie asked.

'It means the name Hugh Cole is linked to Frank Worseley through a third party called Auriol French. Let's look in the

Investigations file.' He pecked at more keys and studied the coded information on the screen. 'That only tells us there was a case that wasn't proceeded with,' he announced. 'We'll have to look in the manual records to find out why.' He stepped down from his seat and went to a filing cabinet. Pulling open a drawer, he hunted through the files and lifted one out. 'Here you are, Sarge.'

Scobie sat down at a desk and began reading. A month ago Auriol French had alleged indecent assault and attempted rape by Frank Worseley, when he was working on the empty house next door to where she lived in Tanniford. The CID officers who investigated the allegations reported that the attack had been witnessed by her mother's brother, Hugh Cole, who happened to call while it was taking place. In questioning Hugh, who was twenty-six, they realized he was mentally retarded, and the case had been referred to the Crown Prosecution Service for advice. The CPS had advised that a defence barrister would easily demolish Hugh's evidence and confuse him. The girl's version of events would be weakened and, in the absence of any other corroborating evidence, the case could not proceed.

Scobie looked up. 'Why didn't this come to light along with the other allegations against Worseley?' he asked the clerk.

'Because no further action was taken, Sarge.'

Scobie booked out the file and took it along to Millson's office. 'I've found a connection between the Habenhowe twins and Worseley,' he told Millson, handing him the file. 'It's a bit indirect, though. Worseley attacked Hugh Cole's niece, Auriol French, a month back. The investigation was dropped because the only witness was Hughie himself, and CPS reckoned the defence would make rings round him because he's backward. The connection with the twins is that they seem to take responsibility for Hughie and he functions as some kind of protector and bodyguard. Perhaps they held a dim view of the police lack of action and took things into their own hands on Hughie's behalf.'

Millson nodded and studied the papers in the file. After a while he grunted. 'More likely it was Cole himself who

142

torched Worseley,' he said. 'I'll bet he's not so daft he can't pour petrol around and set light to it. Let's go grill the three of them.'

CHAPTER 16

Roger North left the office early that Friday afternoon. Charles Howard had already left for New York and Roger planned to spend a quiet weekend in Tanniford on his own after the turbulence of the last two. He took the Tube to his flat in Finchley, packed a bag and set off in his car. He joined the M25 at the time Millson and Scobie reached Pilcox Cottage.

They found no one in and Hughie Cole was not in his caravan. A note pinned to the front door of the cottage gave a telephone number for use in an emergency. Scobie keyed the number on his mobile phone and found himself speaking to the harbourmaster at Titchmarsh marina. After a brief conversation he turned to Millson.

'They put to sea in their motor-cruiser about an hour ago, and they're not due back until early morning. The marina want to know if they should call them up on the radio and ask them to return.'

Millson shook his head. 'Leave a message we want to see them here first thing tomorrow morning.'

The Friday-evening exodus from London had been worse than usual, with the M25 at a standstill in places, and Roger North eventually reached Tanniford at eight o'clock that evening.

He was tired and frustrated by the drive and, after a quick wash and a snack meal, he sauntered down Ferry Street to the Black Dog to unwind over a quiet pint.

Before entering the pub he looked in the car park at the rear to make sure the twins' Saab convertible wasn't there. If it had been he would have walked on down to the quay and along to the Anchor. He'd had more than enough of Georgina and Georgette last weekend.

Stepping away from the bar with his drink, he was startled to see Hughie Cole sitting at a table in the corner. It was unusual to see Hughie in a pub on his own, and the twins had an understanding with the publicans that he would not be served with more than two beers. Hughie was waving and beckoning to him. 'Over 'ere, Rodge,' he called.

It was no use ignoring Hughie. He would simply raise his voice and shout. Reluctantly, Roger carried his drink to Hughie's table. This was not the relaxation he had in mind.

'Where are Georgina and Georgette?' he asked as he sat down.

'Out on the boat.' Hughie took a mouthful of beer and smacked his lips noisily. 'It's called Gee Gee,' he said earnestly. 'G and G for Georgina and Georgette, see?'

'Yes, I know.'

'Gee-gee . . . like 'orses,' Hughie rambled on, ''Cept they don't spell it right. They spell it G-I-G-I.'

'Yes, Hughie, I know all that,' Roger said patiently. His boyhood fear of Hughie Cole had largely disappeared after meeting him again last weekend, but he was still nervous of the lumbering giant's unpredictable reactions. 'Did you want something?'

'What?' Hughie's mouth hung open.

'You called me over. Was it to ask me something?'

'Oh . . . yeah,' said Hughie, remembering. 'When they gonna bury 'im?'

Hughie's thoughts jumped from one subject to another like a grasshopper, and it took Roger a second or two to catch up with this one. 'D'you mean Frank Worseley?'

'Yeah.'

'I don't know. Why?'

'I wanna stamp on 'is grave.'

Roger frowned. 'What have you got against Frank Worseley, Hughie?'

''e done things to young Auriol . . .'orrible things . . . tore 'er clothes an' that.' Hughie stopped, his eyebrows coming together in fierce concentration. The brows parted again.

'Shouldn't've told you.' He reached across the table and laid a great hand over Roger's. 'You won't tell G and G, will you, Rodge? They'd be terrible cross with me.'

Roger went cold as a fearful thought streaked through his mind. He extracted his hand from beneath Hughie's. 'No, I won't tell them, Hughie.'

Hughie Cole drained his glass and stood up. 'Gotta go. Staying with me sister tonight an' she don't like me out late.' He cleaved his way through the crowded bar to the door.

Roger sat gazing into his beer and worrying. Auriol. Pretty, golden-haired Auriol French. Roger had dated her once or twice in his teens ... a shy, 'Don't touch me' sort of girl. He'd been put off by her father who fussed about where they went and what time she came home. And by Hughie, who lived there then, hovering in the background. Roger shivered, imagining Hughie's reaction to Frank Worseley laying his oafish hands on her. He'd beat the daylights out of him. Or maybe he'd told the twins and they'd helped him *kill* Worseley, Roger thought wildly, using him as an alibi.

The door of the pub opened. He looked up and broke out in a sweat. It was the sandy-haired police sergeant. Then he saw an auburn-haired girl with him and recognized Kathy Benson from the estate agent's. He relaxed. For a moment, he'd feared the sergeant had come to find him and arrest him.

At the bar, after he'd bought drinks, Scobie asked Kathy about Auriol French. 'How come she's only a couple of years younger than her uncle, Hughie Cole?'

'Because he was born years later than her mother,' she said. 'Hughie was an accident ... his mother had him in the menopause.'

'Is he fond of Auriol?'

Kathy's brows contracted and she frowned at him suspiciously. 'Why are you asking questions, Norris? Has George Millson put you up to this?'

'No, I'm grilling you on my own account,' he said, smiling.

'That's all right, then,' she said. 'Yes, Hughie is very attached to Auriol. He's like a big brother to her. I don't think she cares for her father much ... if he *is* her father.'

'Lionel French *isn't* her father?'

'Not according to some gossips. It's because Carol left Tanniford one day when she was about seventeen, and returned a year later with three-month-old baby, Auriol, and middle-aged husband, Lionel French.'

On Saturday morning, Millson picked up Scobie from Kathy Benson's flat in Tanniford and drove up the hill to Pilcox Cottage. He was beginning to have doubts about Hughie Cole. It was possible that in the dark his size wasn't apparent because he was hunched over the handlebars, but could he plan that kind of revenge? It needed thinking out. Had he the brain for that?

Hughie Cole appeared at the door of his caravan the moment they stepped inside the front gate.

'He's like a bloomin' great guard dog,' Millson commented as Hughie loped across the grass to reach the cottage door before them.

'I know who you are,' Hughie said, beaming at them and barring their way at the porch.

'Good,' said Millson sourly, 'then tell them we're here.'

Hughie turned and thumped on the door. 'Coppers is 'ere again!' he bawled.

As before, both girls came to the door. They seemed to do everything together, including everyday things like answering the door. Probably went to the loo together, too, Scobie thought comically. They were wearing white slacks and navy-blue T-shirts with their names emblazoned across them in white letters.

They smiled politely. Georgette said, 'Come in,' and Georgina said, 'Off you go to the baker's, Hughie, and get the bread.'

'Just a minute,' Millson said. 'I shall want to ask him some questions, too.'

Georgina's eyes flashed momentarily and then she shrugged and said, 'Stay, Hughie.' He nodded and padded back to his caravan.

Millson and Scobie followed the girls to the lounge and sat down. 'As you know, we're investigating the murder of

Frank Worseley,' Millson began. 'How well did you know him?'

They were sitting side by side on the sofa and Millson directed his question at the space between their heads. He'd had no dealings with identical twins, and the only criminal ones in the records were the Krays, whose details had caused a hiccup on the first police computer. The program had gone into a loop, unable to distinguish between two sets of data containing the same name, initial, date of birth and finger-prints.

Georgina answered first. At least, Scobie wrote in his note-book, that was the name on her T-shirt. 'Not very well. He's been around Tanniford for years.'

'Thick as two short planks, he was,' Georgette added.

'You're aware, I imagine,' Millson said, 'that about a month ago, Hugh Cole's niece, Auriol French, accused Worseley of raping her?'

'We know.' Two copper heads nodded.

'And that the case wasn't proceeded with?'

They nodded again.

'How did you feel about that . . . about the effect on Hugh Cole? You're obviously fond of him. Did it make you mad when we took no action? Did you feel someone should pun-ish Worseley for what he did?' Millson asked.

They stared at him solemnly for a while and then Georgina said, 'Oh, I see,' as though the point of the questions had just dawned on her. 'You think *we* might have set light to Frankie because of what he did to Hughie's niece. Is that it?'

Millson didn't respond. Were they simply being provoca-tive? Or were they trying to fool him? The bold eyes and immobile faces with their identical expressions told him nothing.

'Well, we didn't,' her sister said.

'We're not sorry he's dead, though,' said Georgina.

'Not sorry at all,' said Georgette.

Scobie had warned him of their habit of speaking alter-nately, but he still found it irritating. 'Quite so,' he said, 'which brings me to the bikes in your garage. Someone rode off in this direction on a bike just after the fire started. A

148

bike like those two in your garage. Did either of you ride a bike that evening?'

Their heads shook in unison.

'One of those bikes had mud on the wheels when I saw it early Sunday morning and Hugh Cole told me he cleaned them both the afternoon before. Can you explain that?'

'No,' said Georgette, 'we can't.'

'There's something you should know about us, Chief Inspector,' said Georgina. 'We never go anywhere separately. Ask anyone if they have ever seen one of us without the other.'

'Perhaps Hugh Cole used it then. Perhaps he rode down the hill and set fire to Worseley's place in revenge for what he'd done to his niece, not realizing the man would be trapped and die.'

'Hughie didn't do that,' said Georgette.

'How do you know?'

'We just do!' Georgina snapped.

Millson kept his temper. 'I'd like to ask him about it myself,' he said firmly.

'OK,' said Georgette, 'we'll call him in.' She reached for a handset on the table beside the sofa and pressed one of the buttons.

A few seconds later there was the sound of the back door being flung open. Hugh Cole came charging into the room like a bull elephant. 'Whass up?' he demanded, glaring round the room.

'It's all right, Hughie,' said Georgina. 'These men are going to ask you some questions.'

'I'll speak to him alone, if you don't mind,' Millson said.

'We do mind,' said Georgette. 'Hughie is mentally handicapped and he's entitled to have a responsible adult present when he's questioned by the police.'

Annoyed with himself for overlooking the point, Millson swallowed his pride and said graciously, 'You're quite right. I'm sorry for the oversight. You may stay.'

Scobie turned over his notebook and made an entry on the last page. That was where he kept a record of Millson's rare apologies and even rarer slips in procedure.

'And please could your sergeant put the questions?' Georgina asked.

Millson goggled at her. 'May I ask why?'

'He looks more sympathetic than you,' said Georgette.

Millson stared at her. Then, realizing she was serious and not being provocative, he waved a hand at Scobie. 'Carry on, Norris, you'll probably handle this better than me,' he said magnanimously.

Scobie nodded. Closing his notebook, he leaned forward and said in a friendly tone, 'Sit down, Hughie.'

Hugh Cole sat down gingerly on the edge of a chair.

Speaking slowly, Scobie went on, 'You caught Frank Worseley at your sister's house hurting Auriol, didn't you, Hughie?' Hugh Cole jerked his neck in a nod. 'How did you feel about that?'

'Wanted to bash his head in, but sis said not to touch him else I'd be locked up.'

'D'you always do what your sister says?'

''Course.'

'Can you ride a bike, Hughie?'

'Yeah, 'course I can.'

'Do you ride the bikes in the garage sometimes?'

Hugh Cole's head swivelled towards Georgina and Georgette. Nothing was said and their expressions didn't change, but when Hugh turned his head to Scobie again, it was clear he'd picked up some message from their eyes.

'Yeah . . . sometimes,' Hugh said.

'Did you ride one on Saturday?'

Hugh shook his head vigorously.

'When we were here on Sunday we noticed mud on the wheels of one of the bikes and you told us you'd cleaned them both on Saturday afternoon.'

'Yeah, I did. Polished 'em, too.'

'So, how d'you think that one got dirty.'

There was a sudden rapid exchange between Georgina and Georgette. It sounded gibberish to Scobie, but he saw Hugh Cole's expression change, and knew he'd understood what they'd said.

150

'Ain't got no idea,' Hugh said forcefully. 'P'raps I forgot to clean the wheels.'

Scobie put the question directly. 'Listen carefully, Hughie. Someone poured petrol around Frank Worseley's bed while he was asleep and set fire to him. Did you do that?'

'No.' He answered unconcernedly, in the way of people who don't see the implication in a question.

'Do you know who did?'

There was another sudden exchange of jargon between Georgina and Georgette.

'Be quiet!' Millson said angrily. 'Or else speak properly.'

'We *are* speaking properly,' said Georgina.

'To each other,' said Georgette.

'Then don't!' Millson snapped. 'Or we'll continue the questioning at the police station and have a social worker sit in with him instead of you.' He turned to Hugh Cole. 'Now, answer the sergeant's question, please.'

'Don't know who did it,' said Hugh.

Scobie shrugged his shoulders at Millson. 'I've no more questions,' he said.

Millson regarded Hugh Cole steadily. Was that expression in his eyes vacuousness or innocence? He couldn't tell. 'All right,' he said. 'You can go.'

'Good boy, off you go, Hughie,' said Georgette.

'Is that all?' Georgina asked Millson.

'No, it isn't,' he said irritably. 'I want to know where you two were in the early hours of that Sunday morning.'

'We were here,' said Georgette. 'You know we were. You raked us out of bed.'

'That was at five o'clock. I'm talking about two o'clock in the morning, when the fire started.'

'We were still in bed, of course,' said Georgina.

'With Roger,' Georgette added.

'You can ask him,' said Georgina.

'I will,' Millson said sharply. 'But I shan't place much reliance on what he says because the three of you lied before. North said he was with you the night Trudy Thornton was murdered and you confirmed it. That was a complete fabrication.' He stood up. 'Until I find that cyclist I shan't be satisfied

151

there isn't a connection between the bike in your garage and Worseley's death. Come on, Sergeant. We're not getting anywhere here.'

At the door, Scobie glanced back. Georgina and Georgette remained seated on the sofa wearing expressions like naughty schoolgirls told off by their teacher.

'Let's see if North is here this weekend,' Millson said as he drove down Pilcox Hill.

'He is,' Scobie told him. 'I saw him in the Black Dog yesterday evening. 'D'you think he's involved?'

'I think it's possible they were all in it together. North could have carried out the attack with the two girls acting as his alibi.'

'He doesn't have a motive.'

'Perhaps they had some hold over him. The alibi they gave him for Trudy's murder, for instance. That held good until Sunday when he was forced to admit he was with Laura Howard.'

'I can't see that he'd commit murder rather than admit his affair with her,' Scobie said doubtfully.

'All right, let's say one of the girls did it, and they had him there as their alibi.'

Scobie shook his head. 'They'd hardly murder Worseley for what he did to Auriol French. She's nobody special to them.'

'No, you're right.' Millson nodded gloomily.

Roger North looked fearful when he saw them at the door.

'We're making further enquiries into the murder of Frank Worseley, Mr North,' said Millson. 'And we've just come from questioning the Habenhowe girls.' His hopes rose as North's eyes filled with anxiety. 'May we come in?'

'Yes . . . yes, of course.'

'I'm particularly interested in the cyclist seen leaving Worseley's place just after the fire started. He – or she – hasn't come forward. Now, you told us on Sunday it wasn't you. Do you know who it was?'

'Me?' Roger North spoke with a squeak. 'How should I know? No, I've no idea.'

Millson changed direction. 'The Habenhowe twins say you were in bed with them at the time of the fire. Is that true?'

'Er-yes. Yes, it is.' North was sweating.

Millson nodded. 'Yes, I thought you'd say that. The problem is, Mr North, you told us you were with them the night Trudy Thornton was murdered. It turned out to be a lie. And now the three of you are telling me you were in bed together when Worseley was killed.' His voice became harsh. 'D'you expect me to believe you?'

Roger North swallowed. 'It's the truth, Chief Inspector. Why should I lie?'

'To help them . . . or Hugh Cole. They wanted to punish Worseley for what he did to Auriol French, Cole's niece. Did you know about that?'

'Not until last night when Hughie told me. I wouldn't help Georgina and Georgette over anything, Chief Inspector. Certainly not to cover up a murder.'

'You went to bed with them, though,' Scobie said.

Roger North flinched. 'That was different,' he muttered.

'And you're sure one of them couldn't have cycled down the hill and set fire to Worseley's place?' Millson asked.

'I'm sure.'

He wasn't, though. He wasn't sure at all.

CHAPTER 17

The call came through as Millson stopped outside Kathy's flat, dropping Scobie home.

Two days ago, following the police appeal, a witness had mentioned a saloon car parked near Frank Worseley's house late on Saturday. It had been thought to belong to a visitor to another house, but a diligent woman detective had pursued identification of the vehicle. This morning she had put together descriptions of the driver and the make and colour of the car, and phoned in the information.

Millson's eyes brightened as he listened to the descriptions. Replacing the handset, he laid a restraining hand on Scobie's arm as he was about to get out of the car.

'How many Amazons do you know with shoulder-length blonde hair who drive a dark-blue Mondeo and have a connection with Frank Worseley?' he asked, grinning.

'Only one,' said Scobie.

'Me too,' said Millson, starting the engine. 'I think we've found Worseley's woman visitor.'

The visit from the police, and their questions, magnified Roger North's fears about Georgina and Georgette's real reason for having him there that weekend. They'd duped him with their nonsense about wanting a baby. Knowing he'd be suspicious of a straightforward invite to spend the night with them, they'd used a subterfuge that would appeal to his ego. And he'd fallen for it. He decided to confront them. He had nothing to lose. He went out to his car and drove up the hill to Pilcox Cottage.

They were surprised to see him. 'What do you want, Biggy?' Georgina asked warily.

'I came to see how you were.' For the first time in his life he felt he had the advantage of them. 'I'm an expectant father ... or had you forgotten already?' He smiled wolfishly. 'Did I do the trick? Any morning sickness? Or is it too early for that?'

'Oh, don't be ridiculous, Biggy!' Georgette said crossly. 'You don't think we'd risk getting pregnant, do you? We're on the Pill.'

He gaped at them. The last thing he'd expected was a frank admission. 'So, why make me think you wanted a baby?'

'To get you into bed, of course,' Georgina said. 'You were still on our list. You remember our list, don't you?'

'We knew you'd refuse if we simply invited you,' said Georgette. 'And, anyway, I don't suppose you could perform properly if you were being forced to.'

For a brief moment he almost believed them. Then common sense prevailed. 'I don't believe you,' he said. 'I've just had the police questioning me again. This whole thing – your threat to rat on me to Charles Howard in order to make me spend the night with you – was to provide you with an alibi, wasn't it?'

'An alibi for what?' Georgette asked sharply.

He was about to say 'murder' when he realized they were staring at him intently with that cold, implacable stare of theirs, and thought better of it. 'I don't know. You tell me.'

'Have you told the police this?' Georgina asked.

'No.'

'Very wise,' said Georgette. 'You'd look awfully silly with a story like that. You've admitted you had sex with us, and they're not going to believe we tricked you into it.'

They were right. But they hadn't answered his question. 'So, why did you?'

'We've told you,' Georgina said impatiently. 'It was an excuse to get you into bed.'

They were lying in their beautiful teeth, he thought. They were clever, though. Even that phoney reference to their fertile period had been part of the plan. It had been to explain why he had to be there that particular weekend – the one they'd chosen. And now, in their convoluted way, they had covered over one lot of lies with a further lie.

'I'm flattered,' he said.

'So you should be,' said Georgette. 'Other boys queue up to date us. We thought there must be something wrong with you. But there wasn't, was there?' she said, meeting his eyes.

He gazed into them, tiny lakes of blue, and saw the hint of tenderness. That was when he knew for certain.

Millson had become used to a cold reception at The Lawns and he ignored Laura Howard's hostile expression as she admitted them. She was wearing purple satin trousers and a matching tie-front blouse. In the sitting-room she flicked her hand at some chairs to indicate they could sit down, and seated herself some distance away from them on a chaise longue.

'These frequent visits of yours are beginning to look like harassment, Chief Inspector,' she said, leaning forward to take a cigarette from the silver box on the low table in front of her. 'My husband is in New York, so if this is to do with tittle-tattle from his ex about him and Trudy, you'll have to wait until he gets back.' She closed the cigarette-box without offering it.

'No, this concerns the murder of Frank Worseley.'

'I see.' She lit the cigarette with a table-lighter and relaxed with her arm extended along the backrest of the chaise longue. 'I don't see why you've come to me.'

'A woman answering your description and driving a similar car to yours was seen entering his house around eleven o'clock that evening. Was that you, Mrs Howard?'

She met his eyes boldly. 'Yes. As a matter of fact, it was. When he was here in the morning we discussed redesigning the kitchen. He suggested some improvements, and I went to see him in the evening to finalize them.'

Scobie asked, 'Eleven o'clock is a bit late for a visit, isn't it?'

She drew on her cigarette and blew out smoke through her nostrils. 'Not to me, Sergeant. I'm a night person.'

'How long were you there?' Millson asked.

She shrugged. 'I don't know exactly. He showed me

samples of worktops and things . . . and we had a drink or two, and then I left. I didn't look at the time.'

'Your car was seen leaving about two o'clock.'

She shrugged again. 'Very well, so it was two o'clock. Why ask me if you know?'

Millson turned to Scobie. 'What was the time of the first 999 call, Sergeant?'

Scobie thumbed back the pages of his notebook. 'Seven minutes past two, sir.'

Millson looked hard at Laura Howard and said sternly, 'On your own admission, Mrs Howard, you were at Mr Worseley's place only minutes before the fire was reported. You must see how important that is to us. What were you doing there at that time of the morning?'

Her mouth twisted crookedly. 'Are you deliberately being obtuse, Chief Inspector? Or are you trying to humiliate me? Frank Worseley was a well-equipped, good-looking young man. Perhaps you'd like your good-looking young sergeant to draw a diagram for you.'

'Don't act clever with me!' Millson retorted angrily. 'I'm well aware of the implications. The forensic team found a drinking glass in the bedroom with lipstick on it. What I want is an explanation of your presence there shortly before the fire started, not what you were doing on the bed earlier. Is that clear?'

'Quite clear, thank you,' she said frostily. 'All I can tell you is that that was when I decided to leave and there was no sign of a fire then.'

'What was Mr Worseley doing at that point?'

She looked directly at him. 'Nothing. He was dead drunk on the bed. We'd both had a cigarette and then he fell asleep. And to anticipate your next question, no, I didn't leave a burning cigarette behind. I'm not careless like that.'

Millson pondered her throwaway line about smoking. A double bluff? She must know the room had been drenched in petrol. All the reports said so. Scobie too, bent over his notebook, wondered why she'd said it. Surely Millson would put the obvious question?

Millson did. 'Why didn't you come forward and tell us this

157

before? You must know we were appealing for the woman concerned to identify herself.'

'I didn't, as a matter of fact, Chief Inspector. I make a point of not listening to the news. It's too depressing – always about wars, starving children and murders. And Charles has been away the last few days so I haven't seen a paper.'

Scobie glanced at Laura Howard's face, marvelling at its composure and her air of self-possession. The audacity of her responses to Millson's questions was breathtaking.

She had not taken Millson's breath away. He realized he'd lost the initiative though, as she sat regarding him with slightly raised brows, calmly awaiting his next question. He sought to regain it with a sudden change of direction.

'The last time we were here, you told us the night Trudy was killed you picked up Roger North at Colchester station and spent the night with him.'

'That's right.' Her mouth curved in a half-smile. 'Do I shock you, Chief Inspector?'

'I'm concerned with fact, not morals, Mrs Howard. I'd like you to be specific about times, please.'

She raised one eyebrow and shrugged. 'Roger phoned about half past eleven to say he was catching the two minutes past midnight train from Liverpool Street. He asked me to pick him up at Colchester because the last train to Tanniford had gone. His train was due at one-nineteen, so I must have left here about one o'clock to meet it. I met him and drove to Tanniford, which takes about twenty minutes. Then we had a few drinks and went to bed.' Her eyebrow arched again. 'Is there anything else you'd like to know?'

Millson shook his head.

'What a situation,' Scobie said wonderingly, as they drove away. 'The husband was screwing his secretary, the wife was screwing his assistant, and now we find she was screwing the man who'd screwed the secretary. It's like that play – what was it? *La Ronde*.'

'Instead of moralizing, Norris,' Millson said irritably, 'look for some answers. Two of those characters have been murdered. We have to put the pieces together. They don't fit at the moment.'

'Well, one piece I don't think fits is her explanation for being at Worseley's place,' said Scobie. 'A woman like Laura Howard wouldn't go to bed with a slob like Worseley, whatever his sex appeal.'

'On the contrary, Norris. A woman like her would do just that if she had to.'

'Had to?'

'To keep his mouth shut,' said Millson.

CHAPTER 18

In the line of waiting taxis outside Colchester station on Sunday morning, a bored driver sat in his vehicle listening to the radio. The local announcer was predicting a warm, sunny day. Joe Stebbing decided to give up work for the day and take his wife, Marion, to Clacton.

The weather forecast was followed by further appeals for information on the murders of Trudy Thornton and Frank Worseley. Joe listened with half an ear. He wasn't as interested in murders as Marion was. Marion read crime novels like some women ate chocolates. Couldn't get enough of them. Brought them home eight at a time from the local library. She'd been agog last Friday week when he told her he'd actually had one of the suspects in his taxi that day.

Worseley had flagged him down outside Colchester police station in the afternoon, in a hurry to return to some job he was working on in West Bergholt. He'd been full of his interview with the police, and self-important at being questioned about the murder of Trudy Thornton. 'Helping the police with their enquiries, I was,' he told Joe. To Joe Stebbing it was a polite term for being a suspect and, because his wife was so interested in murder stories, he'd taken note of what Worseley was saying. Now, as the announcer repeated the police appeal, he wondered if Worseley had managed to phone them again before he died. If not . . . Marion would be all ears if he could tell her he'd given vital information to the police.

A moment later Joe Stebbing's taxi drew out of the line of waiting vehicles and headed towards the town.

Earlier that Sunday morning Millson had taken his daughter to the leisure centre on Cowdray Avenue. He sat at the spectators' end of the swimming pool watching her plough up and down the pool. He couldn't read his Sunday paper because she was training for her mile certificate and he'd promised to keep count of the number of lengths. She had completed forty-two when the mobile phone in his jacket pocket began ringing. Unable to hear properly in the echoing noises from the pool, he walked out to the entrance hall to listen.

It was the duty constable in the incident room. 'Sorry to trouble you, sir, but I can't raise Sergeant Scobie. I think his mobile is switched off.'

'Uh-huh. What is it?'

'There's a Joe Stebbing here – a taxi driver – and he's asking for you or Sergeant Scobie, sir.'

'What does he want?'

'He says he was with Worseley when Worseley tried to phone you after his interview here. He thinks the information was important and wants to know if Worseley conveyed it to you before he was killed.'

'He didn't. Keep him there, I'm coming in,' Millson growled.

He glanced through the glass partition into the pool. Dena was standing on the other side in her dripping costume and looking at him distrustfully. The costume clung to her figure and he noticed, with a slight shock, she had developed somewhat since he last saw her stripped. He stepped in through the glass doors.

'You said you'd keep count for me,' she said accusingly.

'I did. You've done forty-two. I've got to go now, love, so you'll have to make your own way home. OK?'

She nodded and he gave her an encouraging smile. One thing Millson appreciated about his daughter was that she never made a fuss over his sudden departures. Her mother would have complained loudly.

Seated in Millson's office, Joe Stebbing explained how Worseley had been in a hurry to return to The Lawns after his interview, and had hailed his taxi outside the police station. He'd been garrulous with relief at not being arrested,

161

and boasted of his conquest of Trudy and making her pregnant. As he told of his refusal to be 'lumbered', as he called it, and Trudy's decision to foist the baby on another man, he suddenly broke off and asked Stebbing to stop at the next phone kiosk.

'He said he'd remembered something,' Stebbing told Millson. 'Something Trudy said that would identify the guy.'

'Did he say what it was?' Millson asked.

'Not then. But he did after he couldn't get hold of you. The way he put it, Trudy said: "You only had me a few minutes, Frank. This man has had me for years and he owes me. We'll let him support me and the baby."' Stebbing paused. 'Those are his words, mind. Anyway, he reckoned you'd work out who she meant from that. So, when I heard more appeals again this morning, I thought perhaps he hadn't told you before he died in the fire.'

'He hadn't,' Millson said, 'and I'm grateful to you for coming in. This information is very helpful. Very helpful indeed.'

Joe Stebbing beamed with pleasure. Wait till he told Marion this.

When Stebbing had left, Millson delved in his pocket and brought out the fresh supply of barley sugar he'd bought when he collected his paper from the newsagent's that morning. He'd planned to ration himself from now on, before he ruined his teeth and added to his waistline. Now, though, he recklessly put three lumps in his mouth at once. He needed to think hard, and this was not the time for self-denial.

Being Sunday, it was quieter than usual around him. He lay back in his chair, closed his eyes and ruminated as he chewed the sweets. Worseley had been loose-mouthed with Stebbing – a complete stranger – and could have been even more so with a friendly and enquiring Laura Howard when he returned to The Lawns that afternoon. Whatever he'd said to her, the consequence had been that she went to his place the following night and had sex with him. Her possible motives, Millson reasoned, were: to discover what he knew . . . or what more he knew; to reward him for not telling the police; to get him drunk and kill him, because at that

162

time the police didn't know of Charles Howard's involvement with Trudy. However, there was no point in killing him to prevent the police finding *that* out unless Howard *had* killed Trudy, which he hadn't. Millson opened his eyes and sat up. *Or unless she had.*

Laura Howard's admission of sex with Worseley hadn't shocked Millson as it had Scobie. He'd asked himself why. Now, he believed he knew. She'd admitted it without batting an eyelid . . . a fearless woman who did exactly what she wanted. 'Ruthless and ambitious' was how Victoria Gill had described her.

'Suppose she found out about Trudy?' he'd asked.

She laughed. 'She'd kill her,' she said, then put her hand to her mouth. 'What have I said! She wouldn't really, Mr Millson. But she'd be pretty merciless.'

Millson reached for his phone and called Scobie's mobile number. It was switched on again.

'Where were you?' Millson demanded.

Scobie sounded sheepish. 'It's Sunday. We were having a late breakfast and didn't want to be disturbed.'

More likely having a romp on the bed, Millson thought. 'I want you in to help me with a reconstruction of Trudy's murder.'

At Kelvedon station Millson drove into the car park and drew up at the passenger exit from the platform. Turning to Scobie, he said, 'Right, the time is three minutes past midnight and a train has just arrived from London. You're Trudy and I'm the killer, OK?'

Scobie nodded and glanced at his watch, then at the platform. 'I come to the exit . . . see your car waiting here . . . walk to it and get in.'

Millson started the engine. 'I tell you we need to talk and drive off towards Feering. Keep a note of the time, Norris.'

When he reached the lane where Trudy had been killed, Millson stopped some fifty yards short of where she had been run down, and reversed into the entrance to a field.

'What do we talk about?' Scobie asked.

'Let's say I try to persuade you to have an abortion.'

163

Scobie nodded. 'I'm intent on having the child, so I refuse.'

'We argue and it develops into a full-scale row.'

Scobie glanced at his watch. 'Lasts at least five minutes, say. Then I can't stand it any longer, or maybe I become frightened, and I jump out of the car and walk off.'

'Off you go, then,' Millson said, as Scobie remained seated. 'This is a reconstruction, remember.'

'OK, but don't make it too realistic,' Scobie said, opening the car door.

Millson grinned sardonically. 'Get on with it, Norris.'

Behind him as he walked away down the lane, Scobie heard Millson start the engine, and then the crunch of tyres as the car came out of the gateway on to the road and began following him. Instinctively, he stopped and turned round. He heard the engine revving as Millson accelerated and, turning back, he began running. There was nowhere to escape to. The banks were high and the hawthorn hedge impenetrable. The car was fast gaining on him. He broke into a sprint and kept on running until he heard Millson's car stop.

Panting heavily, he walked back. Millson had stopped at a blue circle on the road that marked the place where Trudy had been knocked down. 'Hell, you frightened the life out of me!' Scobie gasped.

'I had to make you run faster than Trudy could have done,' Millson said cheerfully. 'It was to prove the killer's car had easily caught up with her at this point. You weren't in any danger, Norris.'

'Supposing I'd tripped? You were right behind me!'

'Well, you didn't, did you? Now . . . you're lying in the road stunned. I reverse and drive over your body to finish you off.'

'You needn't think I'm lying down in the road while you pretend to do that!' Scobie said.

'No, all right. And we'll take the next bit for granted, too,' Millson said.

'You mean the bit where you pick me up and put me in the boot? That's because you can't,' Scobie said with a grin.

'I could if you were Trudy,' Millson retorted. 'But you've made a point, Norris. You've made a point.'

'Which is . . . ?'

'I'll tell you later, when we've finished. How long since Trudy was picked up?'

Scobie looked at his watch. 'Half an hour plus however long the quarrel lasted, if there was one.'

Millson grunted. 'It's working out well. Now I drive your body to the A12 and dump it. Get in.'

Millson turned the car in the next gateway and drove back along Little Tey Road and New Lane to the slip road on to the A12. Parking in the lay-by for the bus stop, he stepped from the car and went to the boot. As he lifted the lid, Scobie joined him.

'You'd need plenty of muscle to lift a dead body out of there,' Scobie said, peering into the deep boot. 'Let alone carry it to the middle of the A12 carriageway.'

'You've already made the point once, Norris, and nearly wrecked the theory I'm working on. Don't keep on about it,' Millson said sourly. 'Time now?'

Scobie consulted his watch again. 'It would have been a few minutes after one o'clock. The lorry driver said he ran over her body at ten past.'

'Right, jump in. Let's see if I can make Colchester station in ten minutes.'

Scobie raised his eyebrows. 'Is this theory of yours that *Laura Howard* killed Trudy?'

'Yes, and I'm not going to explain why until I see if she *could* have done.'

It took fifteen minutes to reach Colchester station. Millson slapped his steering wheel in disappointment. 'She couldn't have made it in time to meet North off the one-nineteen.'

'There would have been less traffic at that time of night,' Scobie said helpfully.

Millson shook his head. 'She still couldn't have managed it – even assuming the quarrel only lasted a few minutes and everything went without a hitch,' he said gloomily. 'But I'd like to try an experiment before I rule her out completely.'

Millson parked in the police yard instead of his usual bay. 'Find me a couple of WPCs,' he told Scobie. 'One about a

165

hundred and twenty pounds and the other the heftiest you can find.'

Scobie went into the building and came out a few minutes later with two uniformed policewomen. One was a tall, hard-faced girl with cropped, blonde hair, similar in build to Laura Howard. The other was a slim dark-haired girl.

Millson had opened his boot and placed a car blanket on the ground by his front wheel. He nodded to the two girls and, pointing to the slim one, said, 'Lie down on the blanket, Constable, and pretend to be a dead body.'

Obediently, the girl lay down on the blanket and smoothed down her skirt.

'And you, Constable,' Millson said to the blonde, 'see if you can pick her up and put her in the boot.'

The blonde girl smiled crookedly. 'No problem,' she said, bending over and seizing the other girl's wrists. With swift, practised movements, she hauled her upright, crouched, and as the girl's body flopped forward, straightened up with her over her shoulder, holding her in place by wrist and ankle.

'It's called a fireman's lift, sir,' she explained. 'No good with a stiff, of course.'

'Nor if you don't know the technique,' Millson said.

'Ah, well, in that case you can do this, sir,' she said, depositing the dark-haired girl on the blanket and pulling her feet apart. Standing between her feet and with her back to her, the blonde stooped and grasped the other girl's ankles. 'Wheelbarrow,' she said, straightening up and hauling the girl towards the boot by her feet.

'Yes, I've got the idea, thank you,' Millson said, as the slim girl's bottom bumped along the ground and her skirt rode up over her thighs. 'How about getting the body into the boot, though?'

'Wouldn't be difficult,' said the blonde. She fetched the blanket and spread it on the ground by the open boot. 'Play dead again, Jackie,' she said.

When Jackie was prone, the blonde policewoman hauled her up by her arms and propped her briefly against the sill of the boot. Then, stooping, she took hold of her ankles and tipped her in backwards. Jackie went into the boot with a shriek and a generous display of her black tights.

'And to get the body out,' the blonde girl said enthusiastically, reaching into the boot and grabbing Jackie's ankles again, 'I'd pull the feet out over the sill and –'

'There's no need to demonstrate, thank you, Constable,' Millson said. Jackie was already looking the worse for wear after the rough handling. 'You've convinced me a woman of your build could handle a body of the constable's weight without much difficulty. Thank you both, you've been a great help.'

The two ill-matched WPCs departed, looking pleased with themselves. Millson stared thoughtfully at the open boot. After a moment he nodded and said, 'She did it, all right.'

'Laura Howard? But I thought we'd proved she couldn't have? She couldn't have put Trudy's body on the A12 after one o'clock and met Roger North at Colchester station at one-nineteen.'

'She lied,' Millson said bluntly. 'And so did he. We'll tackle him first. Come on.'

Roger North went white when he saw them at the door again. After they'd sat down, though, and Millson said his enquiry concerned Trudy Thornton's murder, not Frank Worseley's, his face cleared.

'I want to go over with you again the times and sequence of events after your train arrived at Colchester station that night,' Millson said. 'First of all, what time did the train arrive?'

'It was dead on time – nineteen minutes past one.'

'You said Mrs Howard met you. Where was she? On the platform?'

'No. She was waiting for me in the ticket hall.'

'You're sure about that? She was already there?'

Roger North's throat went dry. Laura had phoned him yesterday evening. 'Darling, the police have been here and I told them a little fib. You remember I was a wee bit late picking you up the night that wretched woman was killed?'

'Yes. Charles had phoned just as you were leaving.'

167

'That's right. Well, I haven't told the police that in case they ask Charles to confirm it, because then he'll know about us. I don't suppose they'll ask you, but if they do, don't let on I was late. I do so want to see you again when this blows over, poppet.'

He'd hung around in the ticket hall for nearly twenty minutes before she arrived, breathless and apologetic. 'Darling!' She flew into his arms and kissed him passionately. 'Darling, I'm sorry I'm late. Charles phoned just as I was leaving, and I couldn't cut him short without making him suspicious.'

'What if he phones again?' Roger asked anxiously.

'He won't.' She laughed. 'I told him I was putting the answerphone on and going to bed.'

It was inconceivable to Roger that this lovely woman could greet him passionately like that shortly after committing murder, and then later make love.

He met Millson's eyes and said confidently, 'Yes, I'm quite sure, Chief Inspector.'

Millson had observed the changing emotions in North's expression, and was sure he wasn't telling the truth. He was also sure Roger North was in love with Laura Howard and would lie for her. There was one way to persuade a lover to betray his love, and Millson took it without hesitation.

'Laura Howard went to bed with Worseley, too, you know.'

Roger North's face froze in surprise and horror. Then he said angrily, 'That's absurd! I don't believe you!'

'Told us so herself,' Millson said, turning to Scobie. 'Isn't that right, Sergeant?'

Scobie nodded reluctantly. He thought it was unethical to reveal that to North.

Roger North frowned, recalling Laura's excuses for not seeing him last weekend. Millson sensed his disbelief faltering and turned the knife. 'Quite open about it, she was,' he went on. 'Said he was good-looking and well-equipped.'

Scobie was aghast at Millson's goading. He didn't understand why Millson was deliberately upsetting Roger North.

Millson's voice turned grave. 'Withholding information

would make you an accessory to murder, son. So, I'll ask you again, and I advise you to consider your answer carefully. Was Mrs Howard with you at twenty past one on the night Trudy Thornton was killed?'

Roger North swallowed. 'No,' he said in a strained voice. Earnestly, he went on, 'You see, Charles phoned just as she was leaving, and she couldn't cut him short and say she had to meet my train, could she? That's why she was late. She didn't mention it to you because you might have checked with Charles and he would have asked why. She's terrified of him finding out about us.'

'She told you this?' Millson asked.

'Yes. And I believe her,' North said stoutly. 'Laura couldn't have killed Trudy. I'd have known. She wouldn't have . . .' He fumbled for words. 'She was her usual self that night.'

'How late was she?'

'About twenty minutes.'

'Thank you.' Millson stood up to leave.

'Where are you going now?' North asked.

Millson raised his eyebrows. 'It's Sunday. I'm going home.'

'You're not going to arrest Laura?' North asked anxiously.

'I don't have any evidence, Mr North.'

'No. I see.' Roger North looked relieved.

'Are you really going home, George?' Scobie asked as Millson drove out of Tanniford.

'Of course I'm not!' Millson snorted. 'I'm hoping that when he phones her – which I'm certain he will – she'll believe we've swallowed her excuse for being late and won't do anything before we get there.'

Cresting the hill, he accelerated sharply. 'Let's have the music on, Norris.'

Scobie reached out and switched on the siren. 'We don't have any evidence against her, though. You said so yourself.'

'The evidence, Norris – the *only* evidence – is in the boot of her car. Hairs from Trudy's head . . . fibres off her clothes. We can't charge her without it.'

CHAPTER 19

At The Lawns, Laura Howard was reassuring a disturbed Roger North who telephoned her as soon as Millson and Scobie left, and plaintively asked about Frank Worseley.

'Darling, of course I didn't go to bed with him,' she said emphatically. 'What do you take me for? I called on him to discuss a new kitchen, that's all. Millson was trying to stir you up. What did you tell him?'

She listened carefully as he recounted his answers to Millson's questions. At the end she said soothingly, 'It's all right, poppet. It doesn't sound as though he's going to ask Charles. If he does, don't worry about it. I'll handle him.'

She put down the phone and sat thinking.

Laura Howard had been incensed when her husband confessed to an affair with his secretary and told her the woman was pregnant. Charles was number two to the permanent secretary and close to the Home Secretary. If the matter became public there would be no knighthood for him, no Lady Howard for her. And they'd be pestered by journalists banging on the door, peering in the windows, and making their lives hell.

She was slightly mollified when he told her the affair had been brief, and he wasn't in love with Trudy. Her immediate concern was to keep it secret.

'Has she told anyone, Charles?'

'No, not even her mother. Trudy knows the mayhem this would cause around the office, and she's anxious to handle the matter discreetly.'

'Can you trust her?'

'Absolutely.' She was as devastated as he was, Charles Howard told her.

Laura wondered. She had met Trudy Thornton a number of times, and spoken to her frequently on the phone. The woman was no shrinking violet.

'What does she propose to do?'

'She intends to resign quietly and go away to have the baby. She promises no one will ever know it's mine.'

'And what does she want from you, Charles?'

'She wants me to support her and the child.'

'Out of the question,' Laura said. 'She must get rid of it. Go somewhere where she won't be known and have an abortion. You'll pay for it, of course.'

'I don't think she'll agree to an abortion,' he said.

Oh, won't she? Laura thought, we'll see about that. Laura wasn't having her glowing future, the future she'd worked hard to achieve, wrecked by a careless secretary's squeamishness. She would speak to Trudy herself, and make her see sense. Bribe her, if necessary.

The opportunity came by chance a few days later. When Charles told her he'd be staying the night in town because of a late-night debate in the House, she'd arranged to spend the night with Roger in Tanniford. That evening, when Roger phoned to ask her to meet him at Colchester, she had a sudden suspicion Charles was meeting Trudy, and asked him if she was still at the party. He told her she'd already left to catch her train home.

Laura decided to meet Trudy's train before meeting Roger's later. If Trudy wasn't on the train it would mean she was with Charles at the flat, and he'd lied about the affair being over. And if she did get off the train, Laura intended to talk to her and persuade her to have an abortion. She would offer to pay for the best possible service in a private clinic and pay her whatever bribe was necessary to keep the matter quiet.

Trudy had been astonished to see her, but had readily agreed to discuss things. Laura had driven to the outskirts of Feering and parked in the first quiet lane she came to.

The discussion had begun amicably with them agreeing it was in everyone's interest to handle the matter discreetly. However, when Trudy refused adamantly even to consider an abortion, Laura became angry.

171

'You can't expect Charles to pay out for the next sixteen years just because of your carelessness in a few nights' fling with him,' she said hotly.

'A few nights' *fling*?' Trudy laughed. 'Is that what he told you? I've been Charles's mistress for years – since before he married you. Oh, there was a break for a few years after he married you, but it didn't last.'

'You're lying!' Laura shouted.

'No, I'm not. Ask him. It's time he paid for all the pleasure he's had out of me.'

'You mercenary bitch!' Laura was beside herself with fury. 'You'll wreck us all!'

'No, I won't. Get a hold of yourself, Mrs Howard,' Trudy said calmly. 'I'll resign from the civil service, and no one need ever know about Charles and me. But I want this child, and he's going to pay for it. And that's all there is to be said. Now, if you'll excuse me, I'm going home.' She jumped out of the car and began walking away.

Laura sat in the car trembling with rage. This trollop had been deceiving her with Charles for years. It was bound to come out about the baby, and that would be the end of her rosy future. Tears of frustration glistened in Laura's eyes. She started the car. She must get the woman back, make her see reason.

When Trudy realized Laura was following her she started running. If she had waited, remained still, Laura thought afterwards, she might not have chased after her and run her down. But her sudden movement had triggered a response, like a mouse exciting a cat, and Laura had stamped on the accelerator, intent now on revenge.

The sudden impact as she smashed into Trudy brought ecstatic release, and for a moment Laura sat in the driving seat, drained of emotion. Then the consequences of what she had done flooded in on her.

She visualized the headlines. 'Top civil servant's secretary run over by wife', in the quality papers; 'Mandarin's mistress mowed down by angry missus', in the tabloids.

She looked around, thinking rapidly. The lane was deserted and there were no dwellings in either direction. She looked at the inert woman lying in the road. There was only one thing to do, and it had to be done quickly. Laura took a deep breath and, clenching her teeth, she drove forward, steering carefully. A sob of anguish escaped her as she felt the front wheels bump over Trudy's body.

Now what? She couldn't leave her here. Where, then? Laura thought of the A12, less than half a mile away. A hit-and-run accident, that's what it would look like.

Stepping swiftly from the car, she dragged the woman's body into the boot and collected her handbag and shoes.

It had taken longer than she expected, though, and she had been late meeting Roger. The chief inspector had found that weak spot in her alibi and now he would pursue it relentlessly.

It had been bad luck, someone killing Worseley the same night she was there. She hadn't taken care not to be seen because there was no reason to. She'd only gone there to find out what he knew and persuade him to keep his mouth shut. As it was, she'd had to humiliate herself in front of those two policemen, and pretend she'd enjoyed having sex with the moron.

Now she must make another sacrifice in order to be safe.

Scobie cut the siren as they approached West Bergholt. Reaching The Lawns, Millson drove fast along the drive to the garage at the rear. On the forecourt, Laura Howard was scouring the boot of her Mondeo with a vacuum cleaner.

Millson climbed from his Rover. 'It's no use, Mrs Howard, that wouldn't remove all the traces of Trudy. Forensic would still find something.'

Her lip curled. 'I know that.' She switched off the cleaner. 'I was going to drive into the country and set fire to the car, then report it stolen.'

Millson nodded. 'That would have worked.' Stepping forward, he said formally, 'Laura Howard, I am arresting you for the murder of Trudy Thornton. You do not have to say anything and . . .'

As he continued the caution, tears welled in Laura Howard's eyes and began running down her cheeks.

'Are you going to charge her with Worseley's murder, too?' Scobie asked as they sat in Millson's office preparing for the interview with Laura Howard.

Millson shook his head. 'The only evidence is circumstantial, and I'm not sure she did kill him. I'm bothered about that cyclist who hasn't come forward.'

'What about the baby? It's ironic she and her husband thought it was his. Are you going to tell her?'

Again Millson shook his head. 'They're going to have a bad enough time as it is.'

'Talking of which,' Scobie said. 'I've discovered where Howard went in his car that night.'

'Where?'

'Kerb-crawling in the King's Cross area. His number was taken by the Met's vice patrol and there's a letter on its way to him.'

Roger North learned of Laura's arrest on the Monday-morning news. He was stunned. There was no mention of Frank Worseley's murder and he wondered again about that night at Pilcox Cottage.

He knew now that the only girl he'd made love to that night had been Georgette. When she left his room, saying it was Georgina's turn now, it was she herself who came in a moment later, not Georgina. He'd suspected it then when he caught a glimpse of her eyes in the moonlight coming through the window. And on Saturday when she looked at him, he knew for sure.

Why had she pretended to be Georgina? Roger wanted to believe it was because Georgina didn't want him, and Georgette was happy to be made love to twice. But a different . . . sinister . . . reason kept intruding into his thoughts.

While Georgette kept him occupied, Georgina could have cycled down the hill with a can of petrol, set fire to Worseley's place, and returned without him being any the wiser.

174

Later in the night, because he'd believed they were up to something, he'd tiptoed to their room to see if one of them was missing. They had been asleep in their beds, lying on their backs, arms crossed on their breasts. The moonlight streaming through the window whitened their faces and darkened their lips, making them look like sleeping vampires.

He shuddered at the memory. It was all too possible. Except . . . he clutched at straws of hope. Except they couldn't have known Frank Worseley would be lying there drunk and helpless, and they had no real reason to kill him.

The newspaper headlines were as sensational as Laura had imagined. Millson found his daughter poring over them when he returned home the next evening. She looked up, with the expression of someone bursting to tell him something.

'Ms Vicki Gill has packed you in,' she said. 'Ditched you. She says the papers are bound to find out she's Charles Howard's ex and start hassling her. She reckons it would be awkward for you if she continued as your cleaner.'

'I see.' Millson sighed. 'Now I'll have to find someone else.'

'No, you won't. She's recommended someone. This one will do fine . . . she's older.'

Millson caught the inflexion in her voice. 'What's that supposed to mean?'

'Well, she won't be after you like Vicki was.'

'She wasn't. You've got a suspicious mind.'

'Comes of having a policeman for a father,' Dena said pertly.

In November, Hugh Cole built a huge bonfire at the bottom of the garden at Pilcox Cottage and Georgina and Georgette made a guy for him. On Bonfire Night, Auriol French joined them and they lit the bonfire and had a barbecue.

The twins had known the truth about Auriol since her mother, Carol, came to them on the day they received the money from their father's insurance. She couldn't tell anyone while Gladys was alive, she explained, and she wouldn't claim a share of the money for Auriol if they did something for Hughie.

'Lionel won't put up with him now he's older, and I'm at my wits' end what to do with him,' she said. 'I can't afford to put him in a home. You must help me.'

'OK, we'll look after him,' said Georgette.

'We'll buy a caravan for him,' said Georgina.

Carol nodded. 'It's a deal,' she said.

As the flames licked the effigy on top of the bonfire Hughie suddenly said, 'Why'dya make him look like Frankie? Did he burn like that?'

'Oh, he burned quicker than that, Hughie,' Georgina said. She had sat on her bike and watched Frank Worseley smash the window ... seen his hair catch fire ... heard him screaming.

The plan had been to pour petrol through the letterbox. But as she arrived there she saw Laura Howard leaving, and the door standing open. Georgina slipped inside and explored. Finding Worseley in a drunken sleep upstairs, she'd poured petrol around his bed and down the stairs to the door, then lit it and dashed back across the road to her cycle.

In the flickering light of the bonfire Georgina and Georgette put their arms round Auriol.

'You're kin ... our blood sister,' said Georgina.

'You've got half Dad's genes, like us,' said Georgette. 'We couldn't let Frank get away with what he did to you. It was like doing it to us.'

''oo killed him then?' Hughie asked.

'Georgie did,' they said together, and laughed.